Marshall Godwin

To Randy

Hope you enjoy!

M Godwin

Felsenmeer Word
35 Bonaventure Avenue, Suite 224
St. John's, NL, A1C 6P2

marshall.godwin@outlook.com
www.felsenmeerword.ca

© Marshall Godwin, 2019

Library and Archives Canada Cataloguing in Publication

Godwin, Marshall, author
On The Wharf / Marshall Godwin

ISBN 978-1-9993912-3-2

Acknowledgements
    Layout and Design by Marshall Godwin
    Beta Reader and Proof Reading: Glenda Godwin
    Editing: Stephanie Porter
    Cover Art: Lindsay Alcock

Published 2019

On The Wharf

Consecution: (Logic) The relation of consequent to antecedent.
Collins English Dictionary

Judgement: punishing the children for the sin of the parents to the third and fourth generation.
Holy Bible, NIV

Consequences: Oh! What a tangled web we weave, when first we practice to deceive.
Sir Walter Scott, Marmion

On The Wharf

All My Family

Chapter 1
On The Wharf
Saturday, June 4, 2016

At dawn, a stillness fills the air. Light from the approaching sun pushes away the darkness, and birdsong welcomes the coming day. In that stillness of dawn, every Saturday morning, Uncle John Parsons and young Johnnie Hawkins met on the government wharf in Port St. William to watch the sun rise out of the ocean.

"Eh, Uncle John."

"Eh, Johnnie."

"How ya doin'?"

"Good b'y. How's yourself?"

"Like the bird."

"Running into windows?"

"What?"

"One of the downsides of being able to fly."

"Jeez, Uncle John, where do you come up with them?"

"Just sayin'. Everything has consequences. Including being like a bird."

"Take the good with the bad, you mean," said

Johnnie.

"Something like that. Make a choice and put up with what happens."

"Where'd that come from this morning, Uncle John?"

"Where everything comes from, Johnnie. A long life lived."

"What are you now, 86?"

"That's right, 86 ... or I will be in three days. I was born in 1930, Johnnie. A long time ago. And you're 16, I believe."

"Turned 16 on May 28. I was born in the year 2000," said Johnnie.

"A good year to be born," said Uncle John. "Makes it easy to keep track of how old you are."

"It does, but to change the subject. You said something about choices. Gotta tell you about Greta Barnes."

"Your girlfriend."

"Well, she was. We broke up."

"How's that? She dump you?"

"No, I dumped her. Well sort of. Before she could dump me."

"Your fault then?"

"Yes, but now I'm not so sure about it. Anyway, let

me tell you about Greta."

****

I liked Greta Barnes, but somehow, I didn't at the same time. Hard to explain. She was too controlling or too sensible or something. Deep down I knew I probably needed that, but it made me feel like I was in a box. I wanted her, but I wanted other girls as well. I suppose I wanted to have my cake and eat it too. That doesn't work with girls. At least not Greta. I suppose I'm a bit wild. I wanted to stay out late, she wanted to go home early. She worried about school and studying, and I wanted to party. We're 16, we're supposed to act like teenagers, is what I think.

Greta is good looking. Slim with a great body. She's hot, you know. But she dresses a bit plain—conservative, I suppose you might say. Her face and body say *wild*. Her clothes and personality say *keep it in control*. It drove me crazy. She's smart too. Smarter than me.

Anyway, Greta and I had been going out for a year. I was proud as a peacock at first – nothing like a hot girl to make a guy feel good. At first, when she didn't seem to want to do much that I considered exciting, I thought it was just because she was shy. Then I realized she wasn't interested in much but sitting, talking, and studying. This is all good, but what about music and dancing and making out? Didn't seem to be that important to her. She also started to get strict with me, and possessive. She didn't like me flirting with other girls or even talking too much with them. I wasn't allowed to have other friends that were girls.

Perhaps I'm making it sound too awful. It wasn't really. We talked about lots of things, she could be very funny sometimes, and she laughed at my jokes. I didn't know what to do. On one hand, I liked her, on the other hand, I felt like I was in a cage. I wanted to run away, but I couldn't bring myself to do it. She was a lady, and I wanted a girlfriend—that was the problem, I suppose.

One day, Leigh Ann and I got talking and laughing and having some fun together. Leigh Ann is another girl in school that I've known for a long time. I always liked her, but we were only ever friends. She started to talk to me a lot more and getting friendly and touching my arm and my hand. I knew she was coming on to me. One day I gave in to the temptation and we kissed. No one was around to see it, but I immediately felt guilty. She said I should leave Greta. I was tempted. Leigh Ann was just the opposite of Greta; she was outgoing, fun, liked to dance, and took chances. You know, like a normal teenager.

I broke up with Greta. She cried and asked why, and I just said I wanted to move on. She asked what that meant, and I said I didn't really know. She pushed me for a reason, and I repeated I didn't know. I got angry and walked away.

I've been with Leigh Ann for two weeks now and we're having a lot of fun, but it seems, I don't know, *thin*. I'm missing the chats Greta and I used to have. But I don't have a chance now with Greta. She has taken up with the smart guy in the grade ahead of us. He's a bit of a geek and we laugh at his ways sometimes, but I think he fits well with Greta. I can tell she likes him. I missed my chance to have a lady. All I have now is a girl.

****

"So, like you said, Uncle John, I made a choice and now I have to put up with the consequences. I have Leigh Ann and we have a lot of fun, and I like it. But it is at the cost of something deeper."

Uncle John thought for a minute. "Yes, but they both lack balance, Johnnie. Life can't be all serious or all fun. You need both.

"I had both once, but I had to make a choice. You

know my first wife's name was Martha. The other woman in this story was named Minnie. She lives up the shore. You wouldn't know her."

"No, I don't think I know a Minnie, and I never met your first wife either. She died before I was born." said Johnnie.

"Yes, that's true." Uncle John thought for a moment and then said, "I wasn't always 86 you know – I was 47 once." He smiled. "Martha and I had two children, twins, Dean and Deanna. They were about 15 years old back in 1977 when this story begins. You know Dean but you probably never met Deanna. But this story is not about my children, it's about me and Minnie. Martha and I were living in Harbour Devon back then."

****

Martha called me from the door of our house. "Suppertime, John!"

I was tying up our boat, a 30-foot trawler-style pleasure boat that we had bought a few years before. I was a fisherman then and had a fishing boat, but it was too stinky for pleasure cruising, so we bought a boat just for our own enjoyment. In Harbour Devon, Martha and I lived on a piece of land that went right down to the seashore. I had a stage and stagehead to dock the boat and to store boat equipment and supplies. Martha and I really enjoyed the boat for summer outings—trips along the shore, sport fishing in season, even spending a week or two on it for vacation. It was completely outfitted with a kitchen, bathroom, and sleeping areas. We loved it.

I finished tying up the boat and went up to the house for supper.

"Did you get the stuff we need?" she asked.

"Yep. Got it all. We'll be ready to go tomorrow when Minnie and Paul get here from up the shore."

Our friends since childhood, Minnie and Paul Kennedy, lived about 3 kilometers by road from Harbour Devon, in a small community called Dorset Cove. They were coming by boat, of course, so that was even closer. They had bought a boat very similar to ours the previous year, and we planned a vacation together that summer: we would travel along the coast for as far as we could get in a week, and then turn around for home. Along the way we planned to dock at community wharfs or anchor in small coves for the nights. There weren't many marinas we could use. We would raft together and enjoy barbecues and music. Paul and I played guitar and the women had great voices. We'd play and sing under the stars.

Paul and Minnie had kids the same age as ours, so we didn't have to worry about them; they didn't really want to come with us anyway and were pretty much independent. We had Martha's sister keep an eye on them, but they were nearly 15 years old and trustworthy. They had summer jobs and Dean had a girlfriend.

The next day we headed out of the harbour, Minnie and Paul leading the way. We got about 50 kilometers before we decided to anchor in a little sheltered cove just a couple of kilometres from Jackman's Arm. The solitude of a small unpopulated haven was better than tying up to a commercial fishing wharf. The weather had been clear all day and it was still nice in the late afternoon when we anchored the two boats together inside the little cove.

I remember that lovely evening and night. The four of us took the small dingy I was towing and paddled in to the beach. We hiked along the beach and up some overgrown trails. Along the way we saw remains of some old houses; just the foundations really. And gaping holes in the sides of grassy mounds that marked where old root cellars had been.

After the hike, we set up our small gas stove and

opened a case of beer. After supper Paul and I got out our guitars and started playing some old favorites. The girls sang along. The sounds of the guitars and singing in the silence of the evening on a secluded beach is wonderful. When the darkness settles in and the stars come out it is even more magical. We made a campfire for light and around midnight we followed the reflection of the fire back out to the boats. The tide, which was almost up to the campfire when we left, continue its relentless flow in over the beach, extinguishing the fire. Then we were off to bed.

    The next morning, we awoke to a dense fog. The air was calm, the water was like glass. The fog stayed all day. Back then there was no GPS, and we didn't have radar, so we stayed where we were. At one point in the day, Paul was taking a nap in his bunk and Martha was asleep down in our bunk. Minnie and I got to chatting. We each had a beer and were sitting on the backs of our respective boats that were still rafted together. We talked for two hours. We'd never had such a chance before. We talked so easily about ourselves and our lives, about what we liked in life, our children, the weather, and what was in the news. I think we could have gone on forever. I got to know Minnie that foggy afternoon better than I had ever known her before. It was intimate, somehow. An intimacy that was broken when Martha came up from down below, rubbing the sleep from her eyes and looking around at the fog still settled in thick around us. I felt a bit guilty and could sense Minnie did too. Not that we had done anything wrong; we had not even left our separate boats. It was just that we both felt the closeness, and it didn't feel quite right.

The next day the fog was gone but wind and rain took its place. It was too nasty to get underway, so we stayed another day in that memorable little cove.

Minnie and I had a few more chances to talk on our boat vacation that summer, but nothing quite like that day in the fog. For the next two years we grabbed every chance we could to meet and talk. They weren't frequent, but they were regular. Then an opportunity arose. I had to go to the city to look at some new fishing gear that had come on the market the same time that Minnie was going to visit her sister. We made love in my hotel room during that trip and after that every chance we got.

Our encounters became more and more risky as time went on, and as we became more daring. We confessed our love for each other, talked about our dreams, told each other it wasn't just about the sex, that it was real love, and it was, I think, for both of us. Thoughts of Minnie consumed my mind. We talked about how we might be together; about leaving our partners; and about how it would affect the children. Eventually my distraction and my changing behaviour made Martha suspicious, although she never said anything directly. I don't think she ever suspected it was Minnie.

And then the crunch time came. I was offered a job here in Port St. William and had to decide. Would we tell our spouses? Would Minnie and I go to Port St. William together, leaving our spouses behind? Would I turn down the job and keep things as they were? Would I break off with Minnie and go with my wife and family to Port St. William and a new life? In the end, that's what I did. I think it was as much a relief for Minnie as it was for me when we made that decision. And we made it together.

We had to make a choice. Would we follow where our hearts wanted us to go, or do what was right? We wanted to run away, to be together forever, to forget about everything else in life, to just hold on to each other and make love. Time tempers love but can never kill it. Minnie still lives down in Harbour Devon. Paul died a while ago.

We made the right choice. Not right for us as two

people in love, but for just about everything else. Right for our children, right for our spouses, right for our future grandchildren, right financially, right in just about every way you can think of. Something was lost and will forever be gone. No one ever knew about our affair as far as we know. We still see each other now and then, and when our eyes meet we know we are still in love somewhere down deep, but the hurt is gone.

We made a choice and there were consequences, but a different choice would have had different consequences, probably worse. We chose the option that led to the most balance in our lives and in the lives of all those around us. We chose balance over love. Some would say we were cowards. Perhaps. But the choice we made was the hard choice. We chose others over ourselves.

****

"That was some story, Uncle John. Don't you think I'm a little young for that stuff?"

Uncle John looked at Johnnie. "I know what you kids watch on TV and in the movies, not to mention what you get into on the internet. I think that story was tame. The main difference is it was real. That's what makes it PG-18."

"I'm only 16," said Johnnie.

"So you are," said Uncle John. "But I told you the story so you can think about balance and the right choices, and consequences of choices. I don't think either one of those girls you hang around with has balance, not yet anyway. Greta is sensible but needs to lighten up, Leigh Ann is carefree but needs to smarten up. You need to keep your mind open. If either of them develops a better balance to life, you would do well with hooking up with her. If not, wait until someone else comes along. In the meantime, work on your own balance and pray that someday the right choice will also be the choice your heart desires."

****

The sun was already well above the horizon when Uncle John and Johnnie walked off the wharf and onto Water Street. They nodded their goodbyes and Johnnie turned left and walked along the street, heading to the south side and up over the hill to his house. Uncle John turned north to begin his morning walk. He was dressed in a warm coat and his salt and pepper hat. It was still cold in the early mornings, even though it was June.

Port St. William's harbour faced east, looking straight

out over the Atlantic Ocean. Port St. William, population 2,000, was still the largest community along this part of the coast. The fish plant that sustained the little town took up most of the north side of the harbour. Most residents worked at the plant or were fishers. The rest worked in the service industries—teachers in the schools; nurses and doctors and others in the small community hospital and clinic; owners and staff of the small grocery store, the hardware store, the restaurants, and fast food places. All the businesses stretched along Water Street. Most of them still had wharfs and storage buildings jutting out over the water, a remnant of days gone by when transportation was by boat. The largest wharf, the government wharf, was in the middle of the business area, looking straight out to sea between the two hills that marked the entrance to Port St. William. Homes were built up the hill behind Water Street or over on the south side.

The other communities dotting the nearby coastline used Port St. William as their service centre. Residents came for health care, to go to school, and to get food and supplies. The only other small town that competed with Port St. William was Harbour Devon, a community of 700, about 20 kilometres further up the coast.

The Port St. William government wharf had been

built decades ago. Back then the coastal boat used to tie up there on its weekly rounds, but it stopped coming when the roads went through. People and supplies moved mainly by road now. Many remembered the old days when the ocean was the lifeline. Things were slower then, thought Uncle John, but more civilized.

    Uncle John walked along the north side to the fish plant and then turned back, walked past the government wharf again, through the business district, and then over to the south side. He looked up the hill toward where Johnnie lived. Uncle John wondered if he would ever have to tell Johnnie the truth about who he was.

Chapter 2
On The Wharf
Saturday, February 18, 2017

"Beautiful sunrise this morning," said Johnnie.

"Yes, bitter cold though. But as long as you dress for it."

"True."

They were both wearing warm winter coats, boots, mittens, and wool caps.

"How long have we been doing this now?" said Uncle John.

"A long time," said Johnnie.

"Can't be that long," said Uncle John.

"Why not."

"You're only 16."

"Will be 17 in a few months."

"Still can't be that long."

"Since last year."

Uncle John thought, and then said, "I've been coming here to watch the sun rise for six years now, since Sarah, your grandmother, died. I suppose I should say I re-started then. I used to watch the sunrise when I was a young boy.

Not always on the wharf. Sometimes on a riverbank or out in a field. Depended on where I lived. But mostly on a wharf, and since I came to Port St. William, on this wharf; and since last year, with you."

"You've watched the sun rise most of your life?"

"I have. I stopped when Martha died, when I was 65. Then I started again six years ago when Sarah died. Every Saturday morning, I imagine I am greeting my two wives as the sun rises. I loved them both, they brought sunshine into my life and I greet them with sunshine once a week. Even if it's cloudy or raining, I greet them. Sunshine is a state of mind, not a weather forecast.

"Wow, you're deep, Uncle John. I remember I came down one Saturday morning to think, and there you were, and there was the sun coming up. I kept coming every Saturday and you were always here."

"Sort of like going to church."

"Yes. You're Father John, and I come for confession."

"Funny boy." Uncle John smiled. "What did you come to think about that first Saturday you wandered down here so early in the morning?"

"I didn't know what to do."

"About what?"

"About Mom's drinking."

"I see."

"She doesn't drink anymore. She used to. Let me tell you about it."

****

"I'm home," I shouted every day after school, as I closed the door behind me. Mom didn't answer. I would find her in the same place every day. Sitting on the sofa asleep in front of the TV, with an empty drink glass on the coffee table beside her. Snoring. I woke her up with a touch on the shoulder. "Mom wake up. I'm home."

It took a second shake to get her awake. She grunted a little and looked towards me. "Hi, Johnnie," she said. "You're home. Sorry I was asleep."

"You're asleep every day when I get home, mom," I said.

"Sorry, Johnnie. I get tired in the afternoon."

"From what?" I asked.

"Don't lip me now, Johnnie."

"You don't do anything. How can you be tired?"

"More lip, Johnnie."

"I'm just saying, mom. The house is a mess and the breakfast dishes are still in the sink."

She stumbled to her feet, and said, "You help me clean up now Johnnie. Like a good boy."

I helped mom clean up before dad got home. She stopped drinking and made supper; it was ready when dad got home. Most of the time dad didn't know she was drinking, but he did catch her sometimes. They would argue about it. Sometimes at night I could hear them downstairs after I went to bed.

After a while, the afternoon pattern changed, and I would arrive home and she wouldn't be there. I would start to clean up the house and in half an hour or so she would come home. I could smell drink on her.

"Where have you been?"

"Visiting a friend," she would say.

"Which friend?"

"No one you know. Thanks for getting started with the cleanup. I'll make supper now."

Some days she wouldn't get home in time to make supper, and dad would get home and wonder where she was. I would have the dishes done.

"Has she been home since you got home?" he'd ask.

"No," I would say, "But she did say something about going to visit Aunt Jean today, remember?"

Of course, mom wouldn't have said any such thing, I was just covering for her and I didn't know why.

That night there would be more arguing downstairs.

Then dad started going out after supper and mom started drinking in the evenings. If dad wasn't around, she would drink, that was the pattern. She started drinking more because he wasn't around as much. The arguing got worse. Most days she was hardly home at all, and most evenings he wasn't home. I was looking after myself a lot and I was only 14.

Then we got a call from the hospital. Mom had fallen and broken her leg coming down the stairs in Jim Pike's house. She hadn't had any clothes on. She had to be sent to the city to have surgery on the bone in her leg. She got sick in hospital with shakes and seizures and seeing crazy things. They said she was an alcoholic. Dad spent the whole time in hospital with her.

After that they stopped going out by themselves and mom stopped drinking. She goes to AA now. Things are a lot better and she's always there when I get home. Dad stays home at night now and there is no more arguing.

****

"They lost their way," said Uncle John.

"Yes, I guess they did," said Johnnie.

"But you're lucky, Johnnie. They found their way back and you still have a family."

"Yes, I guess you're right."

"Often when people lose their way, they don't find their way back. They get lost forever. Let me tell you a story."

****

I suppose we lost our way physically as well, but it was more than that. We truly got on the wrong track in life. Or at least I did.

I was young; in my early 20s. I was away from home for the first time and I knew no one – except Fred Hawkins who had come with me to Toronto. The day after I arrived in Toronto by train from Halifax, I started looking for work and I found a job as a dish washer in a Chinese restaurant downtown. Not a fancy restaurant, but that didn't matter, I had a job and would be able to pay for my room and board at Mrs. Wong's house where I stayed.

Mrs. Wong's daughter, Chen, still lived at home. She

was two years younger than me and worked in the family laundry business. While Mr. and Mrs. Wong's English wasn't very good, Chen's was excellent. She was born and raised in Toronto and had gone to English schools. I ate with the family and had to get used to some very different foods. Rice wasn't a major part of the Newfoundland diet, while they ate a lot of it – with some sauce, and bits and pieces of vegetables, and meat I didn't recognize sometimes. Chen apologized for the food one evening; not because she didn't like it herself, but she realized it was different for me. They all ate with chopsticks but were gracious enough to give me a fork and knife. However, it didn't take long for me to get used to using the chopsticks.

  My bedroom was at one end of the house, Chen's was at the other end, and Mr. and Mrs. Wong slept in the room in the middle. Sometimes Mrs. Wong would point at Chen and then point her finger at me and shake it, and then shake her head and say, "No, No." I knew what she was getting at and so did Chen — she'd look at me and laugh whenever her mother made sure I knew she was forbidden fruit.

  I had been at the Wong's for nearly three weeks when my bedroom door opened one night, and Chen walked in. She quickly removed the light nightgown she was wearing and got in bed with me. It all happened so quickly I was a bit shocked. I jumped out of bed on the other side, slowed only by the fact that she had me by my private parts. I managed to pull away and stood there with my hands covering what had just been held on to, and said, "Chen, you're a no-no, remember."

"They're sound asleep, John. They won't hear a thing. And don't you think I am worth the risk?"

She was out of bed, standing up on the other side, with not a stitch of clothes on and looking very beautiful and very tempting indeed. But I took her by the arm and led her to the door. It creaked as I opened it. I pushed her out and threw her nightgown after her. "I'm too afraid, Chen," I said.

She came to my room again the next night and the night after that. On the third night I lost my way, and my virginity. I was a very naïve boy from the bay. Chen, who was two years younger than I, was not a virgin.

We had to keep our relationship secret because her parents would have killed me. Not to mention her older brothers, who came by to visit now and then, and always looked at me suspiciously. I started going out in the evenings so they would think I had a life outside of their family, which I didn't really. Later, Chen would say she was going to spend some time with a friend, and we would meet downtown, in the seedy district where the restaurant I worked in was — but we didn't meet in that restaurant, because Chen's grandfather was the owner. Mostly we walked around the streets and went to some shows. Chen loved just hanging out and holding hands.

Somehow, friends of Chen's brothers found out we were going out. They threatened they would tell on us if we didn't help them with something, but they wouldn't tell us what.

"We'll tell you when you need to know," a big Chinese man a few years older than me said. He grabbed me by the arm. "You understand? You say nothing. You and your girl show up back here on Saturday night. Eight o'clock. If you don't show, I'll tell her brothers you're with their little sister. They kill you slowly."

I didn't want any part of being killed slowly, so on Saturday night at 8 p.m. we were at the same place on the same street, waiting. They showed up only to say they were testing us and there was nothing for us to do, but we were to be back there again the next Saturday night. A few more comments about dying slowly kept me motivated, and so the next Saturday we were both there again, on time and wondering what would happen.

After a while we saw two men walking towards us. One turned his head a little and put his finger up to his lips as if to say: "stay quiet."

We did. As he went by, really close to me, I felt his hand go in my jacket pocket, and he said, "walk away."

I took Chen by the arm. We walked down the street and crossed at an intersection. Just as we did, two other men came running up the street in the direction where the two Chinese men had gone. I steered Chen into a small alley between two buildings. It was getting dark. I put my hand in my jacket pocket and pulled out a large bracelet ringed with what looked like diamonds. We stared at each other. There was also a note. It read: *Go to the restaurant where you work.*

"We can't go there together," said Chen. "Someone I know may see us. I will go first. You follow after five minutes and sit at a different table."

We did as she suggested. When I got to the restaurant, I could see Chen sitting over in the corner. I sat in the opposite corner and a waiter I recognized gave me a note. I looked at him questioningly. He shook his head and walked away.

The note read: *Come to kitchen. Bring it.*

As soon as I went through the door to the kitchen, the cook, a big sumo wrestler sized man, grabbed me, walked me over to the back room, and pushed me in. Inside, Chen's grandfather sat in a chair, flanked by the two Chinese thugs who had threatened Chen and me.

"Give me," said the elderly man.

I took the bracelet out of my pocket and handed it to him. He took $100 from his wallet and gave it to me and said, "Go. When we need you again we will tell you. Be good to my granddaughter."

I looked at him, shocked. Shocked because a $100 was a lot of money, and also because I realized he knew I was going out with his granddaughter.

"Go," he said again.

I turned and left as fast as I could. I walked out the door and a few minutes later Chen left. We met on a corner two blocks away.

"It was your grandfather," I said. "He gave me $100 and he knows about us."

"Oh my God, do you think he will tell my parents?"

"I don't think so, not as long as I do what he says. He said he would need my services again and I don't think he meant washing dishes."

Chen and I served as the drop-off point many times after that. Same pattern, different locations. The transfers happened quickly, and the follow-up was always in the backroom of Wong's Diner. Chen's grandfather was always there. And he always reminded me he knew about his granddaughter and me.

This had me in a bad spot. I was making a lot of money — they paid me $100 for each delivery. The merchandise was usually jewelry but sometimes it was bags of white powder, which I knew must be opium or something like that. I didn't care and didn't ask. I just accepted the money and kept doing what I was asked to do.

I didn't know how I could ever get out. What if I wanted to go home? Would they let me? I didn't think so. I knew too much for them to just let me go.

I was trapped. I didn't know which way to run, where to go, where to turn. It was like being in the woods and not knowing which way to go to get home. I had lost my way.

So, I did nothing, at least nothing to find my way. I just kept being the drop-off boy. I offered Chen half of the money her grandfather was paying me, but she didn't want any. Then one day, about two months after this started, my world was turned upside down.

"John, I want to tell you about Peter, Peter Zhang. My boyfriend," she said.

I looked at her and like a fool said, "My name is John, I'm your boyfriend."

"John, I always knew about the things my grandfather did, my brothers know about you and me; it's only my parents that do not. They truly are just two Chinese business people who run a laundry and dry-cleaning service."

"My God, if your brothers know, why haven't they come after me?"

"We set you up. I was the bait. The threat was the trap to get you to do what we wanted. But I'm not needed here anymore; you are so involved now that if you try to leave they will kill you, and if you go to the police they would say you are part of it, as you are."

It all started to make sense. "So, you do have a boyfriend named Peter. And you mean he knows what we have been up to?"

"We all do what we have to do for the family. But what we have been doing for the past few months has been very pleasant, don't you think?" She touched my hand; I pulled away.

Things got a lot cooler around the house after that,

and I was very awkward around Chen. She stopped coming to my room, of course. I would see her and Peter around town now and then. I avoided them if I could. Once when I saw them, I thought Chen was pregnant, but I couldn't be sure.

The drops increased from weekly, to twice a week, to most nights. I had trouble fitting in my shifts at the restaurant. Then after one of the drops, when I was delivering the package to the back room, grandfather Wong said to me, "You too busy to work in kitchen now. We need you as fulltime middleman. Your pay now $115 each package so you don't need to work in the kitchen. OK?"

It was OK, of course. I hated washing dishes. The extra $15 per drop would add up to more than I was making at the restaurant anyway. "OK," I said. Then quickly, perhaps too quickly, I asked, "Can I go home for Christmas?"

"No Christmas," he said, louder than usual. "You with us now, you stay in Toronto, or my nephews kill you slowly."

There was that threat again. As Chen had said, she was just the bait; once I was in the trap, they had many ways to keep me there.

I opened a bank account and soon had thousands of

dollars saved. I was rich by my standards, but I couldn't make much use of it. You can't spend money when you're lost in the woods—at least I couldn't spend it on what I wanted to spend it on, like a boat and a house in Newfoundland.

I finally made a good decision. I started to wire money to my mother at home in Harbour Devon and asked her to deposit it into an account for me. I kept just enough in the Toronto bank to live off. I lived well, mind you. Mother asked me once what I was working at to make so much money. I told her I'd tell her when I got home.

Then one evening, about three months after Chen dumped me, it all came crashing down. We were caught red-handed by the police just as the big Chinese man was making the pass to me. They came out of nowhere, and they had guns. The Chinese man drew a gun and was shot before he could do anything else; I dropped to the ground. shouting, "Don't shoot."

The fun was over. Money stopped flowing and I was in jail, held until the case went to court. The police spent a long time questioning me about my role in the scheme. I agreed to tell them everything I knew in return for some leniency. In the end, I got two years in the medium security penitentiary in Collins Bay just outside Kingston, Ontario. Grandfather Wong and his nephews got five years each, but Grandfather died before he could finish his time. Mr. and Mrs. Wong were investigated but never charged.

Chen escaped charges too. Later I heard she had been sleeping with a policeman who was investigating the case. Anything for the family, I guess. Peter Zhang, Chen's boyfriend, disappeared. Nobody knew where he went.

****

"You spent time in prison!" Johnnie was surprised.

"Yes, I did, and some time I'll tell you stories from the two years I was there."

"Wow. You're an ex-con."

"Yes, I am. But you're making it sound like it's something glamorous. Believe me, it's not. The reason I told you the story is to show you how easy it is to get lost — to be seduced. Your mother was seduced by alcohol and both your parents by the lure of a new or different relationship, thinking the one they had was not working. Rather than working on what they have, people think the grass is greener in another pasture. Sometimes when you get lost in life, only a crisis can help you find your way back.

"For your mother, for both your parents, I guess, it was her embarrassing fall and the broken leg. For me, the seduction had been money and a woman. The fear of a slow death kept me trapped. But alcohol is no less a trap and no less a seduction. My only way out was through prison, for your mother it was through the hospital. We were both lost, and the way back home was through the doors of an institution. We both needed help to find our way. People who don't discover that, or don't have it thrust upon them, stay lost forever."

"You made a lot of money, though, Uncle John."

"Yes, I did, Johnnie, and I'll tell you about that sometime as well."

"You mentioned my grandfather, Fred Hawkins, went with you to Toronto. He died before I was born. I never knew him," said Johnnie.

"I know," said Uncle John, and left it at that.

"The sun is getting up in the sky," Johnnie said as he gazed out over the water towards the east. "China is out that way isn't it? In the east, I mean?"

"Yes, I suppose it is. But it's in the opposite direction, too. On this round earth you can get anywhere from two completely opposite directions. When you travel and you are halfway around the world, it is then that you are also halfway home. Have a good day, Johnnie."

"You too, Uncle John."

****

Uncle John Parsons walked off the government wharf and turned right, toward the fish plant. It was a cold winter morning and he wore a grey toque, a Canada Goose jacket his son, Dean, had given him a few years before, and a pair of sealskin winter boots and sealskin mittens. In the spring he wore a grey peaked cap on his head. It was only in the summer you could see his bald head. By his mid-50s, Uncle John had lost most of his hair. He was thin, fit, and sinewy; the way most men are who make it to his age.

Along the way he noticed a few fishermen going into their stages, probably to do some preparatory work for the coming spring and the next fishing season. Fishing was a seasonal industry in most of Newfoundland, usually lasting from April to November at the most. Uncle John noticed Spencer Hawkins open the door to Brett Dawe's stage. He could see Brett in the stage through a window. Uncle John's son Dean was married to Betty Dawe; Brett was her brother. Brett and Spencer had been good friends since their 20s.

Uncle John decided to pop into the stage as well to see what they were up to.

"Eh, Uncle John," said Brett when he saw who had opened the door. The light of the sun and the cold air poured in; both suddenly blocked when Uncle John closed the door.

"Eh, Brett. Eh, Spencer," said Uncle John. "What's everybody up to these long cold days of winter?"

"Same as every year," said Brett. "Mending the gear, maintenance on the boat, keeping an eye on what the government is up to about quotas and other regulation changes. It's different every year it seems."

"How's school going, Spencer?" asked Uncle John. Spencer was a high school teacher. He had moved up to principal the previous September. Spencer was Sarah and Fred Hawkins son – although there was more to that story. Uncle John hoped he would never have to tell the rest of the story. He hoped he could take it to his grave.

"Not bad," said Spencer. "I like my new job. Hopefully I can flow right into retirement in about 15 years."

"I suppose you're nearly 50 by now, aren't you Spencer?"

"I'm 48."

"Has it been that long?" Uncle John mumbled.

"What?" said Spencer.

"Oh, just musing about how time flies," said Uncle John.

"Brett, I was saying before Uncle John came in, have you heard anything about the ferry to Redman Island? I heard the government was going to shut it down."

"I wouldn't be surprised they're thinking that way, but I haven't heard. There's only about 20 people living out there now. Can't see how the government can afford to keep providing basic services. The people should move. Come here to Port St. William or to Harbour Devon. Their kids would be better off."

"Most of them are fishermen," said Uncle John. "They'd be a long way from their fishing grounds. They'd have to fish around here. Wouldn't that interfere with you, Brett, and the other local fishermen?"

"It might," said Brett, "but they could still fish out around Redman Island. They just might have to stay out there for several days at a time or something like that."

"Yes, I suppose," said Uncle John.

"You and Johnnie still meeting on the government wharf every Saturday," said Spencer, more a statement than a question.

"Yes, we are," said Uncle John. "Just came from there now."

"Yes, I heard Johnnie go out the door this morning. It was still dark."

"We usually arrive down on the wharf 10 or 15 minutes before sunrise."

"What do you guys talk about, Uncle John?"

"You name it. Johnnie is a wonderful young man. He thinks deeply about things."

"Like what?" asked Spencer.

"You know, we talk about life and relationships. And I tell him about my life and where I've been."

"Like you being in Dorchester when you were a young man," laughed Brett, breaking into the conversation.

"No, we haven't talked a lot about that," said Uncle John, a little taken aback by the comment. "And it wasn't Dorchester, it was a medium security penitentiary in Ontario. Collins Bay Penitentiary was the name."

"Whatever, Uncle John. You're an ex-con, right."

"Yes, that's true, I am. Always will be, I guess. Well, I think I'll be on my way." Uncle John walked to the door.

"I think I'll be going as well," Spencer said. "Bye Brett."

"Sorry about that," said Spencer when they were both outside on the road. "There was no need for Brett to bring that up."

"Brett has been like that towards me for many years now, since he and Dean had a falling out. He never did like the fact that Dean married his sister."

"Well it's pretty damn rude of him anyway."

"Thanks Spencer, but I've had to deal with a lot more than that in my lifetime. See you around."

"See you, Uncle John. Do you know if Johnnie headed home after you left the wharf?"

"Well, he headed that way. That's all I can say."

"OK, thanks. Bye."

Chapter 3
Fred Hawkins

At 21 and 22 years old, Fred Hawkins and John Parsons arrived in St. John's in 1952 on the *Glencoe*. The next thing they had to do was find passage on a boat to Halifax where they could catch a train to Toronto.

"Let's find a place to stay," said John. "I need some rest."

"Yes, b'y perhaps you're right," said Fred. "We were told to look for Marian's Boarding House. Wonder where it is?"

"Up on Queen's Road," said a voice behind them. "I'm Jack Wadley from Belleoram. Sounds like you fellars are from the outports somewhere? Just got off the *Glencoe*, right? So, you must be from the south coast."

"Thanks. Which way to Queen's Road?" asked John.

"I'll walk ya up there," offered Jack. "That's the easiest thing to do."

"You live in St. John's now then? Working here?" asked Fred.

"Yes, I works on the docks loading ships bound for all over the world. Places I never been meself. Boston and over in England and Portugal. All over. Down to Jamaica even. Hopes to travel them places someday. But for now, well, I got to make some money. Come on let me show you where Marian's place is."

"Have you stayed there yourself?" asked John.

"When I first came here. It's the cheapest place. And if you're like I was, every penny counts. Beds are a bit lumpy, but the food is good. "She says she got rid of the bed bugs."

"Jaysus," said Fred. "Bed bugs. Is there a better place to go?"

"You could stay at the Newfoundland Hotel, but you'll pay 10 times as much."

"Ah, b'y, Fred. Let's take our chances with the little critters," said John.

Fred and John shared a bed. Next morning, they accused each other of snoring, but realized shortly after it was the guy in the next room. Walls were thin.

"Don't think I got any bites," said Fred.

"Me neither. But let's get downstairs to breakfast and then go find passage to Halifax."

****

On August 14, 1952, they took the passenger ship *Nea Hellas* to Halifax and disembarked at Pier 21. They were Canadian citizens, had been since Newfoundland joined Canada in 1949, so there was no fuss with immigration.

"Let's ask that guy directions to the train station," said John, pointing to a man inside a booth.

Before John could get a word out, the man barked, "What do you want?"

"Looking for the train station," said John, put off by the gruffness of the man.

"You're Newfies," he said.

"Yes b'y," said Fred. "I'm from Port St. William and John here is from Harbour Devon."

"I don't give a damn where you're from. Newfie is enough for me. Train station is that way," he pointed to his right. "You leavin' Nova Scotia?"

"Yes, goin' to Toronto," said John.

"Good."

John had to hold Fred back. The man laughed. John pulled Fred toward where the man had indicated.

"If all Nova Scotians are like that fellar, I'm glad we're off to Toronto," said John.

"You should have let me at him," said Fred.

"Just would have got us in trouble, Fred."

"I suppose. I wonder if people in Toronto are any better?"

"Probably not," said John. "We're just Newfies to Canadians."

"We're supposed to be Canadians now," said Fred.

"It'll be 100 years before we're anything more than Newfies to them. Just you wait and see."

"Ya tinks day tinks we talks funny?" asked Fred. He could put on a strong Newfoundland accent when he wanted to.

"Might be," said John.

****

Two days later Fred and John lugged their bags off the train in Union Station. A man on the train told them a good low-price hotel in Toronto near Union Station was called the Royal York. He said it had an uppity name, but it wasn't too bad at all.

They got a taxi to the Royal York and the taxi driver stopped after about 30 seconds and said, "Here you are."

A few minutes later they discovered the Royal York

was in fact the most expensive hotel in Toronto.

Dragging their bags out of the lobby of the Royal York, armed with the name of a hotel the concierge had kindly called and booked for them, they waved down another taxi. Ten minutes later, they went through a door much smaller than the one at the Royal York and paid for a night in a shared room.

No obvious bedbugs on inspection of the bed, and toilets seemed to work. They fell into bed with their clothes on and were asleep in minutes.

The next morning, they bought newspapers, checked the classifieds for jobs, and started making calls at the coin phone outside the hotel. Several times they went back into the hotel to get change. John got lucky, and that first day he got a job in a Chinese restaurant and was also able to stay with the owners of a laundromat who took in boarders. The job was enough to pay for his room and board, and still have some left over. His father had always told him to try to save 10 per cent of everything he made, and John planned to do just that. Fred was still on the phone, job hunting, when John left in a taxi for Chinatown. He gave Fred the name and number to the Chinese restaurant and said to call him once he was settled.

****

John kept Fred up to date on how he was doing and his relationship with Chen Wong. Fred decided he wanted to meet this Chen girl and arranged to meet the couple in a restaurant in Chinatown – not the one John worked at. This was before John got tangled up with Chen's grandfather's illegal business.

Chen and John were sitting at a table in the back of the restaurant when Fred walked in.

"Hi Fred, good to see you." John shook Fred's hand. Then he looked to Chen, and said, "Chen, this is Fred Hawkins, my best friend. Fred, meet my girlfriend, Chen Wong."

"Nice to meet you, Chen," said Fred. He shook her hand and was obviously stuck on the girl.

"Have a seat, Fred. John, you have a very handsome friend. I like him already," Chen smiled at Fred.

"Well, let's not get too carried away here," John laughed. "You're with me, remember."

"Of course," she said, still looking at Fred and smiling.

Fred was getting uncomfortable. He turned away from Chen and toward John and said, "How've things been with you? Apart from hooking up with Chen, of course. I know that's been a good thing." He couldn't believe it. He had wanted to get the conversation away from Chen and instead he had brought it right back to her.

"Yes, I think I have been a good thing for John. Don't you think John? We are good together, right?"

"Yes, we are," said John. "Chen and I are having lots of fun getting to know each other. I've been telling her about home and she tells me about her family and what it's like growing up in Toronto as a Chinese person. They have very tight families."

"John my man, did you just say they have very tight fannies?"

"No, no, I said tight families. You know, like close families."

"What does fannies mean?" asked Chen.

John blushed. "It means your bum, your buttocks."

"Oh, my ass," said Chen. "John did you say I had a very tight bum?" She smiled at him and laughed. "Just joking with you, John. And you did say *family*, not *fanny*. Fred is just playing with you, aren't you Fred?"

"Yes, I was. Nice to get you all riled up and embarrassed though." He laughed and patted John on the shoulder.

John wasn't sure he still felt Fred was his best friend, but he laughed anyway, then stopped abruptly and gave Fred a look.

They chatted for about an hour. By the end it was mainly Fred and Chen talking. After Fred left to walk home, Chen looked at John and said. "No need to worry John. I'm your girlfriend."

Not long after that was the first meeting with Chen's cousins and her grandfather, and John was caught in the trap.

****

The guard opened the door to the small room and let John in.

"Sit on the chair and keep your hands up on the countertop, visible at all times," said the guard.

John sat, put his hands up on the counter, and looked through the glass barrier at Fred Hawkins. "Hi Fred. I was surprised when I heard it was you. What's up?"

"I just wanted to see how you were doing."

"I'm OK, I guess. As good as you can be, locked up. I have a quarter of my time served and I'm just trying to keep my head down and behave."

"Well you're looking OK. I got a job on the lake boats, but you know that. It's a good job. I'm on the boats for three months and then a month off to go back home for a while. I'm at the end of my second contract right now. Just got off the boat. I'll be heading home tomorrow. I'm still going out with Sarah White. You know Sarah."

"Yes, I know Sarah. She's a good friend. How is she?" asked John.

"She's doing great, John, but I have to tell you something. After I heard Chen broke up with you, I looked her up. She told me she had a Chinese boyfriend, but that she liked having a white man boyfriend. That's the way she put it. We got together on several occasions. I'm sorry John. I really am. Anyway, Chen got pregnant. She said it was me or Peter Zhang's. She said she wouldn't know until the baby was born. I know it isn't the policemen she fucked to get herself out of trouble, because she was already pregnant when he came on the scene. It's not yours or she would have had the baby a lot earlier than she did. Anyway, she had a baby girl. She called her Susie. She says the baby is definitely mine because it is part white."

"Jesus, Fred. What are you doing?" said John.

"I'm not doing anything, John, and she says she wants

nothing to do with me even though I said I'd help her out. She says she doesn't want any man's help. Once she asked if I knew how you were doing. I told her I hadn't been over to Kingston to visit you yet. If I'm talking to her again, I'll tell her you are doing fine and say hello. Should I?"

"Don't say anything about me, Fred. And I really don't care that you went out with her. That whole part of my life is something I want to forget. I just want to get back to Newfoundland."

"OK, fair enough."

"But Fred. What are you doing to Sarah? You know our families are close. Here you are up here screwing around and probably have fathered a child. You're still trying to contact that woman, and I'm sure you would have sex with her if she was willing to get back with you. Stop stringing Sarah along. When you go back home, you make a decision. If you want to stay with Sarah, go back home after every three-month contract and don't stop in Toronto for a piece on the way. If you don't treat her right, I swear I'll take her from you and marry her myself. Do you hear me? I swear I will tell her what you have been up to."

"Jesus, John, don't do that," said Fred.

"Stop playing her. I know Sarah loves you, but I

won't have her being hurt. You stop the shit you're up to, or I'll tell her everything when I get out of here."

"OK, John, I will, I promise."

With that, Fred got up and left.

John considered writing Sarah and telling her but decided against it. He would give Fred a chance.

Chapter 4
On The Wharf
Saturday, May 27, 2017

Johnnie sat on the edge of the wharf and gazed eastward. He could make out the dark outlines of the two headlands that formed the harbour entrance. The first flash of the sun would come soon, rising out of the water on the distant horizon. The birds were singing.

Where was Uncle John? Johnnie hoped he wouldn't miss the sunrise. That would be strange. Johnnie had sometimes been late and missed the sunrise, but not Uncle John.

At the very moment the sun was about to slide up from the ocean and into the sky, Uncle John stepped on the wharf and waved. "Just in time," he said. "Looks like a great one this morning. The haze will make it bright red, I think."

Johnnie smiled. Uncle John could always be trusted to be on time. "Come sit," said Johnnie.

The two of them sat silently, legs dangling over the edge of the wharf, watching the red sun rise. It was the eve of Johnnie's 17th birthday. They had known each other for most of Johnnie's years, but it was not until the past two they had grown close. Uncle John had been married to Johnnie's grandmother Sarah, his dad's mother, for 10 years until she died six years ago. That had been Uncle John's second marriage.

"You almost didn't make it in time this morning," said Johnnie.

"It's about timing. I knew I would make it right at the minute of sunrise. Like you, I check each night to see when sunrise will be, so I know when to be down here. I've been doing this so long I know exactly how long it takes me to get here."

"I guess it takes you longer now to get down to the wharf than it did 30 years ago."

"It does. I've had to adjust my timing."

"I don't eat breakfast before I come. Do you?"

"A cup of tea and a piece of toast every morning before I go out the door," said Uncle John. "Even when Martha was still alive, I would get that for myself, but by the time I got back up to the house she would have porridge made for me."

"Mom makes breakfast for me weekdays before I go to school, but weekends I'm on my own. It gives her a break and she can sleep in. Things have been so much better the past year since she stopped drinking. I always boil eggs on weekends. I can never quite get the timing right. I like them hard but just hard, not overdone."

"You need to use Martha Stewart's technique. Put the eggs in cold water in a pot, bring them to a boil, and just as they start to boil you take them off the heat and wait 13 minutes. Voila – perfect hard-boiled eggs."

"Where do you learn all this stuff?"

"I watch too much daytime TV since Sarah died. But look at the sky this morning, Johnnie. Unusual pink and purples. Don't see that a lot."

Johnnie looked at the colours for a while and then said, "There's something I'd like to tell you about. Remember Greta and Leigh Anne?"

"I do. Balance and all."

"Well, it's not about them, it's about their younger sisters. After I broke up with Greta, you will recall I started going out with Leigh Ann. But after our talk, I decided to break off with Leigh Ann as well and become a free agent. That went along fine for a while until Greta's sister, Rita, and Leigh Ann's sister, Jody, both started to show an interest in me at the same time. Rita and Jody are both 15; I feel like I'm robbing the cradle."

Uncle John stared at him and chuckled, "Robbing the cradle? You're all still in the cradle from where I'm standing"

"Sure, but there's something about being almost 17 – my birthday is tomorrow. I can't explain it, but it's like they're too young."

"Don't worry about it. When you're 86 and almost 87, and they're 85, you won't notice the difference at all. Anyway, tell me what's going on."

****

They're good friends, Rita and Jody. I saw them talking, whispering, and looking at me and laughing. At first, I thought they were making fun of me, but then they started coming over to me and getting friendly. They complimented me and said nice things. It was like one was always trying to outdo the other when it came to having the final word. The school bell might ring, and Rita would say, "See you after class, Johnnie" and Jody would say, "Can't wait, Johnnie," and Rita would say, "Wait for you forever, Johnnie." And Jody would say, "Me too, Johnnie." And it goes on like that.

It makes me feel good, but saying it out loud, it sounds stupid.

Anyway, I think I like Jody the best but I'm not sure why. If I asked Jody to do something with me, Rita would be upset, I'm sure. So, I decided I would only to do things with them together. Not really go out with either of them, but always do things as a group.

I like trouting. I've always liked trouting. Doug and I were planning to go trouting a few weekends ago. Then Doug sprained his ankle in the gym and couldn't walk on it very well. I really wanted to go trouting and I was going to ask Bill, but then I thought it would be a great chance to do something with Rita and Jody. I didn't think they would go, but I gave it a try.

"Want to go trouting with me?" I asked one day at recess.

They looked at each other, and then looked at me, and in unison said, "who?" Wondering who I was talking to.

"Both of you," I said.

I wasn't sure if the look on their faces was surprise, disappointment at not being the chosen one, or dismay. They both professed their love for trouting, said they knew all about it, said their fathers had taken them many times. I didn't believe a word of it, but we agreed to meet up by the Fisherman's Lodge at 8 a.m. Saturday and head in the trail to

Three Island Pond.

At five minutes to eight I was in the parking lot outside the Fisherman's Lodge. It was a little chilly, so I had dressed in a fleece with my fishing vest over it. The forecast didn't call for rain, so I hadn't bothered with rain gear. I had my hip rubbers rolled down below my knees for walking, and I carried my spin-cast rod with a flip back reel in my right hand and, over my left shoulder, a small backpack containing some lunch, extra fishing tackle, and a container of worms for bait. After a little while I looked down the hill to see Jody and Rita huffing and puffing up to the parking lot.

"You're wearing runners!" I said with surprise. "And you've got pushbutton reels ... and bobbers for god sakes!"

"What's wrong with pushbutton reels?" asked Rita. Jody asked the same question with her eyes. "And we don't plan to go in the water anyway; we'll fish from the shore, so we don't need big heavy rubbers."

"Oh my god," I said. "You two sure you've been trouting before?"

"Sure, lots of times," said Jody. "Don't be an asshole now. Let's get started."

"OK," I said. "Let's go. Should be there in an hour or so."

I could tell they wanted to say something, but they didn't and just fell in line behind me on the trail. It was dry and flat and wide for the first 10 minutes or so, then we came to the first muddy boggy part as the trail went down into a small valley. I just walked on through the swampy ground and turned and looked back. The girls were both still on the other side, trying to figure out how to get around the wet spot.

"What are we supposed to do?" Jody whined. "I don't plan to walk in that fucking water." Jody didn't have much of a filter.

"Go around it, in the bushes on the left side, and you should be OK," I said.

The girls didn't look too sure. They were wearing capris and probably worried the bushes would scratch their legs. Which is exactly what happened. They got to the other side of the 10-foot stretch of muddy bog, dry but with a few scratches. Jody came out cursing me and Rita looked a bit frightened. I kept my mouth shut and led the way along the path. By the time we reached Three Island Pond their runners were muddy and wet.

"What kind of trouting trip is this?" Jody said, as they stumbled out of the last few bushes that had overgrown the trail next to the pond and onto a flat rock on the shore.

"The only kind I know," I said.

"We usually go trouting on the side of the road. Dad drives out the highway, stops by his favourite pond, and we go trouting," said Rita.

"And do you catch anything?" I asked.

"Sometimes," she said.

"Well, here I guarantee you will catch lots of trout. You have to work for it, but you get results."

The girls were delighted with the results. Once we started catching fish they didn't even seem to mind when they had to get their feet wet to get around some parts of the shore. By noon we had each caught 10 trout of our quota of 12 trout per person. We decided to stop at a clear area by the shore and have lunch. After about 20 minutes of eating lunch, chatting, laughing, and enjoying the sun—which had become warmer as the day progressed—Jody said she was going to move further down the shore and see if she could catch her final two trout. Rita and I stayed on the dry grassy patch where we had eaten lunch. One thing led to another and before we knew it we were making out. We were kissing and I started to move my hand across her chest to her breasts. She said, "No!"

I said "What?"

"Don't touch me there. You can touch me anywhere else."

I move my hand down on her belly and as it got lower, she said, "Don't touch me there."

"You said anywhere else."

"I didn't mean there."

"OK," I said. We kissed for a while longer and then we heard Jody coming back, so we straightened ourselves up and when she came into the open, we said in unison, "You catch anything?"

"Just one," she said.

"I think I'll go and try my luck," said Rita. "Want to come with me, Johnnie?"

"No, I think I'll stay and keep Jody company," I said. Rita glowered at me but went on up the shore and out of sight. Before I could catch my breath, Jody was on me. She kissed me and took my hand and put it on her breast. I helped myself to the delight. Then she took my hand and put it between her legs and put her hand down between my legs. It was all too fast. I moved away and stood up. "I'm sorry," I said. "I think we should stop."

She laughed at me. "Johnnie, you've never done that

with a girl before have you? You're a virgin. I'm not and I can teach you a lot."

I grabbed my fishing pole and went down the shore in the opposite direction from where Rita had gone. I just needed to get away from both of them.

****

"Johnnie, you're being pretty frank with me. Aren't you afraid I'll tell your parents?" said Uncle John.

"Well you've told me some things over the months that wouldn't sound good if I told people," said Johnnie.

"True," said Uncle John. "I tell you what, let's make a deal. Ever been to Las Vegas, Johnnie?"

"No," said Johnnie.

"Well in Vegas there's a saying – *what happens in Vegas, stays in Vegas*. So, let's agree, *what gets said on the wharf, stays on the wharf*. We're free to tell each other anything. You OK with that?"

"Perfect," said Johnnie. "It's a deal."

"Timing," said Uncle John.

"What?" said Johnnie.

"It's all about timing, Johnnie. You got the timing wrong with Rita, and Jody got the timing wrong with you."

"Yes, I suppose you could look at it that way."

"I had a problem with timing once," said Uncle John. "Want to hear about it?"

"Sure."

****

Having done my time in the Collin's Bay penitentiary, I was on the second last leg of my journey home. The *Glencoe* rounded the northern headland and turned into Port St. William harbour. I was in my 20s and my best friend, Sam Ryan, was waiting to greet me on the dock as the passenger boat settled in sideways to the wharf and was fastened securely with large ropes.

"John, great to see you." Sam shook my hand and then embraced me. "It's been a long time. Welcome back and thanks for keeping in touch with your letters. I appreciated them."

"Hi Sam," I said. "It's great to be back. How're you doing? How are your parents?"

"Everybody is fine. Let me help you." A large trunk had been offloaded and was sitting on the wharf. We both took a handle and carried it to the waiting truck; the only one in the little community at that time. It would take me on the final leg of my journey home – down to Harbour Devon, about 20 kilometres away. Sam jumped into the middle of the front seat and I sat by the window. A tight squeeze, but not a problem. Sam had come up from Harbour Devon in the truck to meet me at the dock.

It took nearly an hour to travel the distance over a gravel road full of potholes and ruts. I was paying the driver as my mother and father came running out of the house to greet me.

Two days later, I was settled into my parents' house in Harbour Devon, a temporary stop until I could decide what to do with my life. After I was home for a week, Sam and I took a small boat to Port St. Williams and I checked in at the bank. There was no bank in Harbour Devon in those days. My account had $20,000, accumulated from my time in Toronto. In the 1950s a teacher made about $700 a year and a really good salary was $3000 per year. I was a wealthy man. What to do with it, was the question.

"I could help you spend it," Sam joked. "I need a new pair of shoes."

"Well I'm sure I could get you a pair of shoes," I smiled back, "Wouldn't want you to get a blister from a hole in your sole."

"My soul is just fine." I recognized the play on words.

Sam taught at the little school in our town. All grades from kindergarten to Grade 11 with a total of 13 students. Thirty dollars a month bought room and board and the remaining $30 from the monthly salary of $60 was for everything else.

"I get by," said Sam. "I even try to put $5 a month away in savings. After two years teaching I have about $100 in the bank. Nothing compared to your stash—Perhaps I should go to Toronto and make my fortune, like you."

"Wouldn't recommend it," I said. "More to life than money."

"That's what people with lots of money always say."

"I suppose," I said.

I played with the idea of sharing my wealth with Sam, perhaps $1000 or so, but I decided I would wait.

Samantha Penelope Ryan was her full name, but everybody called her Sam. If there ever was a girl you would call a tomboy, it was Sam. I don't think I ever saw her in a dress or skirt, always in trousers, which was unusual for the 1950s. We had grown up together, best friends since we were toddlers. After high school, Sam completed six weeks summer school at Memorial University College in St. John's and came back home to teach. I left and went to Ontario. We had written each other regularly while I was away, just to keep in touch, including while I was in jail. I thought Sam would have found a man and married, but she hadn't even had a boyfriend.

There was something different about Sam, I didn't know what it was. Growing up in a small fishing community we didn't really know about homosexuality. I'm not even sure the words *gay* and *lesbian* were used then, certainly not by us. The word *queer* was used in a derogatory way although it was years before I knew what it really meant. In a small community of less than 1,000 people I'm not even sure there was another woman around like Sam, I don't think there was anyone close enough to her age who she could have connected with. To me she was just Sam, a woman I should have started having feelings for long before I did.

A few months after I arrived back home, I was missing real female companionship, and I got to thinking about Sam. It was hard to think about Sam that way though. She never dressed to be sexually attractive, always wearing loose clothes, you could never make out the shape of her breasts or the curve of her hips. Then one summer day, Sam and I went fly fishing down in Famieux Bay where a salmon river flowed into the ocean. We each caught a salmon in the morning, but by noon it was so warm and humid we started taking off clothes. After a while Sam had had enough and she undressed right down to her birthday suit and jumped in the water. I was dumbfounded. I had never seen her naked before. She was absolutely beautiful. Sam was a strong swimmer and swam straight out from the boat; as her arms swung over her head, one after the other, the water swirled around the nape of her neck and her bottom rose up and down out of the water as she kicked her legs. After about 100 feet she rolled over on her back and I could see her breasts and the black patch of hair between her legs. She waved to me, "Come in," she said.

I pulled off my clothes, embarrassingly revealing my erection, and jumped in the water. It didn't take long for the cold water to take the life out of my penis. I swam out to her and she grabbed me and pulled me close and kissed me on the lips. I was startled at first, but soon was kissing her back. We swam back to the boat and made love.

"I've never been with a man before," she said. "I'm glad it was you."

I didn't know what to say. I was too shocked about what had just happened.

"I had a girlfriend in Toronto," I said. "I was with her."

"Yes, I know," she said. "You told me all about that in your letters, remember?"

"Yes, right. Of course."

Sam looked at me and said, "I had a girlfriend in town when I was attending teacher's college, John."

I looked at her, not really understanding what she meant at first. Girls having girlfriends usually meant having a friend that was a girl. Then it dawned on me what she was saying. I didn't know what to do or what to say. I felt awkward, and I said awkwardly, "So you are that way. I mean always that way. You like women and not men."

"I don't know what I am, John. I can't be always that way because what we just did was wonderful. I enjoyed it, and I think I have feelings for you. But I feel urges towards women as well."

"Sam," I said, "I have feelings for you too, but they are all mixed up, even before you told me what you just told me. Mainly because I have always seen you as a good friend. Almost like a sister. But I have to admit that recently I have been thinking about you a lot 'that way' if you know what I mean."

"Is it possible to be good friends, and to be lovers? Even though I am drawn towards women, I do want to have children, John. And I would like you to be their father."

This whole thing was racing along so fast I didn't know what to say. I eventually said, "Let's head home, Sam, and think about this."

There was disappointment in her eyes when I said that. I didn't really mean anything negative, I just needed time to comprehend what she was saying. It was as if she had just asked me to marry her a few minutes after she told me she was a lesbian.

We didn't say much on the way back in the boat. I started the engine and manned the rudder in the stern. Sam sat in the bow. That picture of her sitting on the thwart in the bow facing the wind, now and then looking back at me and smiling, is how I remember her.

Sam hung herself that night. She left a note in an envelope addressed to me saying she loved me but that our lives together would be a nightmare because she needed more than I could give her, and I would always feel as if I was second fiddle to women. It took me a long time to get over Sam. I did love her in many different ways. Two years later I met Martha and the impact of Sam's tragic ending faded, but

I have never forgotten her.

I still have the letter she wrote me. No one has ever seen it and you are the only one who knows about it. Even Martha, God rest her soul, never knew about Sam.

"What gets said on the wharf stays on the wharf, my young friend," Uncle John finished. Johnnie was silent.

They got up to walk off the wharf and Uncle John said, "By the way, Johnnie, I won't be here next Saturday, I'll be in St. John's. An old friend died and I'm going to his funeral. See you Saturday after next."

"OK," said Johnnie.

****

When Uncle John walked off the wharf that morning he didn't turn right and start his morning walk around Port St. William, he went back to his house. Uncle John lived in a two-story saltbox house, painted dark mustard, the colour dories are often painted, with a red trim. Uncle John and Martha had bought the house in 1980 when they moved from Harbour Devon to Port St. William. They lived there until Martha died in 1995. Five years after Martha died, John married Sarah Hawkins and they spent their married life in the house until she died in 2010. Both of his wives died in that house, in the same bed. John contemplated moving after Sarah's death, but the house held memories of his two wives, so he stayed.

His old 2002 GMC Sierra pickup was parked by the house. There was lots of rust on its body, but it started with the first turn of the key. Sort of like himself, Uncle John thought. He left Port St. William and headed down the road to Harbour Devon. The road was in much better shape than it had been in 1952 when he arrived back home from Ontario. He covered the 20 kilometres over the paved road in 20 minutes. Uncle John didn't drive fast.

The shed where Sam had left him the letter and then disappeared from his life forever was long gone. Her father had torn it down in the 1960s. He walked up over the field and sat on a rock near to where the shed had been. He had done this a number of times over the years. Whenever something caused him to remember Sam, he would make a pilgrimage to this spot. Telling the story to young Johnnie had triggered the need to quietly sit, look out over the water of Harbour Devon, and recall that time he had fallen in love with and made love to Samantha Penelope Ryan.

An hour later Uncle John was heading back to Port St. William in his truck.

Chapter 5
On The Wharf
Saturday, July 15, 2017

"It's pouring rain, I'm soaked," said Johnnie, as Uncle John stepped out on the wharf about two months after the *what stays on the wharf* agreement.

"With the amount of rain we get here in Port St. William, it should be raining more often on Saturday mornings than it does. Have you noticed how we almost always get to see the sun come up? Days like this, where it's rainy or cloudy seem to be fewer than they should be. For some reason the odds of a rainy Saturday morning seem to be less than our weather pattern would suggest."

"Good luck, I suppose," said Johnnie, "But we're paying for it today."

Uncle John pulled out an umbrella. "Most days this wouldn't work with the wind we get here, but today the rain is coming down straight."

"Don't have another one of those, do you?"

"Actually, I do," said Uncle John as he pulled a telescoping umbrella out of his pocket and handed it to Johnnie. He had brought an extra one along this morning thinking it would be needed.

"Wow! You actually do have another one. Thanks."

"It's the Boy Scout in me. Always prepared." Uncle John smiled.

With both of them under an umbrella, they looked at each other, and laughed. "No sunrise today, I guess," said Johnnie.

"Just because we won't see it, doesn't mean it won't happen."

"True." Johnnie and Uncle John were quiet for a while. "Remember a couple of months ago I told you the story about Rita and Jody, and you told me about Sam?"

"Yes, I remember," said Uncle John.

"I'm seventeen now. Going into grade 12 in September."

"Yes, I know," said Uncle john, wondering where this conversation was going.

"I'm still a virgin you know."

"No, I didn't know. Is this going to be another one of those *it stays on the wharf* mornings?"

"I don't think so. My life hasn't been too exciting lately. School is just out and I'm going to be working on the fish plant for the summer, starting Monday."

"You got a job? That's good."

"Yes, anyone who wants a job on the plant can get one if they're willing to do anything that's asked of them. I'll be a labourer. I'll have to do whatever kind of manual work they ask me to do."

"Good for character building," said Uncle John. "I had a job once that was sort of like that."

"I feel a story coming on," said Johnnie.

****

In September 1959, Martha and I had been married for four months. I was in my late 20s and Martha was three years younger. No children. I didn't have a permanent job. We were living off my savings, which I didn't want to do, so we decided to move to the city to see if one or both of us could get work.

St. John's was a quaint place back in the '50s and '60s, even by the standards of the '50s and '60s. We stayed in a boarding house for a week or two and then found a place to rent on Merrymeeting Road. Martha got a job at the Browning Department Store downtown and I found work as an elevator operator at the Hotel Newfoundland. I pretty much spent my day pushing buttons, taking people up and down the floors at the hotel. It was easy, but god it was boring.

Anyway, while I went up and down in the elevator at the fanciest hotel in the city, Martha went up and up in the high-end retail business. Within two months she was head of her department and by six months she was responsible for inventory purchasing for several departments. In May she was asked to go with the manager to New York to choose and buy stock. She travelled a lot for several months and then one day out of the blue she said she wanted to go home.

"What?" I said, not expecting that at all. "You have a great job here. You go places, you're making three times the amount I make, why do you want to go home?"

"Because I love you, John, and I'm afraid of what will happen."

She said her manager, Bradley Browning, son of the store's founder, was a nice man. But he was starting to come on to her. First, he complimented her a lot, then he started buying her things, and eventually he asked her if she would come back to his room with him during one of their purchasing trips. She refused, she said, but it was hard for her to be upset with him because he was so nice to her. She decided the only way out of the situation, and the only way to make sure she would never give in to his overtures, was to just go home.

I wasn't quite sure what to think of it all. On one hand I felt good that although Bradley Browning had much more to offer Martha than I would ever have, she chose to stay faithful to me. On the other hand, I guess I was a little upset that the temptation was so great she had to take drastic measures. In a sense I had come out on top despite overwhelming odds.

Martha died of breast cancer when she was 62, I suppose you know. I looked after her during the last six months which she spent in bed mostly. It was a hard death for her. I did what I could. Those months will haunt me forever. Ten years after Martha died, Bradley Browning was in Port St. William for some reason that I don't recall now. He came to visit me. He said he wanted to apologize for the affair he had had with my wife those many years ago in St. John's, and that she had made the right decision to break it off and stay with me. He said he had been heartbroken but, in the end, it was for the best – he eventually found another woman he loved, and they married and had children. He said he was glad she had a good life with a good man like me.

Well, I wasn't quite sure what to do or say when he

told me this. I had always understood that there had never been an actual affair in St. John's, just his attempt to get Martha to sleep with him that she had rebuked. I didn't challenge him, but simply accepted his apology and he went on his way. He obviously thought Martha had told me about an "affair" and that we had worked things out and stayed together.

What do I believe? Do I believe Martha's version of the story and hold on to my own belief that she was faithful and chose me? Or do I believe Mr. Browning's story? Perhaps it doesn't matter. Martha might have been in a similar situation as I was with Minnie. We both faltered, we both lost our way for a while, but we eventually both made the decision to stay with the marriage. I had loved Minnie, perhaps Martha had loved Bradley, but the love we had for each other was different. A love that persisted despite the odds, and despite the human weaknesses that sometimes cause us to fail.

****

"Not sure how that fits in with me telling you I had a job at the fish plant doing manual labour." said Johnnie.

"Well, maybe it's a stretch," said Uncle John. He

smiled. "I was thinking about the overwhelming odds that a young man who got a job at the fish plant, and started getting used to making good money and having money to spend and perhaps buy an old car, would end up quitting school and staying at the fish plant. Many young men and women a few decades ago fell into that trap, and perhaps they still do today.

"Finish high school and go to university or college, Johnnie. The money will feel good now, but it won't last, or at least the joy of working at the fish plant won't last, even if the love of money does."

"I am planning to be an engineer, Uncle John," said Johnny. "I don't think I'm the sort to work at the fish plant all my life."

"Good," said Uncle John. "Not that working at the fish plant is something to be looked down upon. It's just that if you can do better you should. In the meantime, it's a good way to get used to working, and making and managing money."

"Think I'll buy an old Mustang."

"Stop it," Uncle John smiled, and gave him a gentle bat on the head.

The rain had stopped. The sun was out. It was already

On The Wharf

well above the horizon.

****

Johnnie and Uncle John walked off the wharf onto the road and went their separate ways. Johnnie worked at the fish plant Monday to Friday, although he did have to work some Saturdays depending on when the large offshore fishing boats came in to offload their catch. The boats were often gone for a week or two before they returned. This Saturday there were no boats expected, so he was off.

Johnnie had gotten his driver's licence a few months before and he and Leigh Ann were going to the Salmon Festival in Grand Falls. It had taken some convincing to get his parents to agree that he could take the car, drive 300 kilometres to Grand Falls, and stay for two days, including an overnight in a hotel with a girl. Johnnie promised to drive carefully, said they would have separate bedrooms, that they were just good friends—but it hadn't worked. Spencer Hawkins was still too worried to agree to the trip. They called a family conference.

Spencer, Mary, and Johnnie, and Leigh Ann and her mother and father met at the local diner, had supper, and talked. It was close, and it was only when Johnnie pulled the final ace from his hand that they agreed to let them go to the concert. Bill White, Johnnie's friend, who was a year older, and Bill's girlfriend, Greta Barnes, would also be going with them. Greta had such a reputation for compliance with rules and general "goodness" that their parents agreed. The four would leave early Saturday morning and drive back Sunday evening. It was a three-hour trip each way. There were 10 different musical performers. The band they wanted to see was on the Saturday night.

Johnnie and Leigh Ann were friends. Although they had been an item for a few months the year before, now they were just buddies and neither had any intention of changing their relationship. Leigh Ann and Greta were not good friends. They had never really liked each other, and when her parents seemed to suggest that Greta and Bill be in charge because Bill was older and Greta was more mature, she was totally pissed.

When Johnnie arrived up at his house after leaving the wharf, Leigh Ann, Greta, and Bill were already there and ready to leave. Johnnie grabbed his backpack, kissed his parents, and jumped in the car behind the steering wheel.

Three hours later they had checked in to a small motel in Grand Falls. They took two rooms, one for Bill and Johnnie and one for Leigh Ann and Greta. Greta said she had no intention of staying overnight with Bill. She would go visit him while Johnnie visited Leigh Ann in the girl's room, but she intended to sleep in the girl's room. She had made that very clear.

Johnnie and Leigh Ann said that was fine with them. Bill seemed disappointed. But Greta was doing the mature thing, as promised, and Johnnie knew it was because of Greta's ways that he was even on this trip in the first place. Same old Greta, he thought. All proper and no fun. Lack of balance he could hear Uncle John say.

The show was great. Afterward, Leigh Ann and Johnnie talked for a few hours in the girl's room while Greta and Bill made out in the boy's room. Johnnie wasn't sure what Greta and Bill were doing though. Greta totally forbade any alcohol or drugs be brought in the rooms. Johnnie thought perhaps they were having sex, but he kind of doubted it.

"We've only got one more year before high school finishes and we have to decide what we're going to do. You still thinking about engineering?" Leigh Ann asked Johnnie as she opened a can of Pepsi and poured it into a glass.

"I think so, but the trip the principal has planned, where we all go to St. John's this fall and get introduced to all the programs that Memorial has to offer, might change my mind. Who knows? I'll see." Johnnie popped the tab off a Pepsi can and took a big swallow. He liked it better that way, rather than in a glass. "What about you? You mentioned nursing a few months ago."

"Medicine. I've decided I'll see if I can get into medical school. I know I want something in health care, so I figure *in for a penny in for pound* as my grandma says."

"Wow. A doctor. But I can see it. Your marks are good enough for sure, even with all the partying you do?"

"I've cut back a bit on that now. Matured, you might say. Not quite like Greta though. I wonder what Greta plans to do?"

"Who knows," said Johnnie. "An astronaut maybe." They both laughed. The laughter caused them to fall towards each other on the sofa. Johnnie pulled back. Leigh Ann looked embarrassed.

"I'm sorry," he said.

"No problem. But I think we're past that." They both nodded in agreement." And besides, Johnnie, I've seen you and Charlotte Parsons spending some time together. She really likes you you know."

"Yeah, I like Charlotte, too."

"I'll always consider you a good friend, Johnnie."

"Likewise," said Johnnie looking at her. "Give me a hug."

They hugged, and Leigh said, "Let's see what's on TV."

Chapter 6
On The Wharf
Saturday, February 10, 2018

"I miss some Saturday mornings in the winter," said Johnnie.

"I know. Why is that?" asked Uncle John.

"Not sure. You would think with the sunrise being later I would be less likely to miss it. But when it's still dark outside in the morning and you know it's cold, you just want to snuggle under the covers and go back to sleep. And because of the weather, too. It's hard to even think about getting up and going down to the wharf if it's blowing and snowing and you know the wind will cut right through you. I just want to stay in bed those mornings."

"I miss some mornings too," Uncle John said. "Like you said, if there's a snowstorm, or freezing rain, or it's just plain cold and miserable, I might just turn over and catch an extra 40 winks. The sun still seems to rise without me."

"I've never been here when you weren't," said Johnnie.

"I don't miss many."

"It's cold this morning," said Johnnie. "Minus 12, I

think."

"Yes, cold," said Uncle John, "but clear. Like a day I remember in Goose Bay, Labrador. Although it was much colder, about -25 degrees, if I recall correctly."

"A story about Goose Bay coming, Uncle John?"

"No, just thinking how bitter cold a day can be – a cold that could kill if you were exposed too long – and yet clear and sunny with a sparklingly beautiful blue sky. The contrast of the dangerous cold in the midst of beauty. It reminds me of how different two people can be. Take my children Dean and Deanna. Dean was always outgoing and active. He grabbed life with both hands and shook it hard. Deanna was quiet, reserved, didn't say much, stayed in her room and read. The thoughtful sort. It always struck me how two children who were formed and grew in the same womb at the same time could be so different."

"Yes, I suppose," said Johnnie. "You would know."

"Remember the story I told you about Martha and Bradley Browning."

"Yes."

"I should tell you about something that happened about 20 years later."

****

In May 1982, shortly after coming home from St. John's and their second year of studies at Memorial University, Dean and Deanna asked to meet with me alone when their mother wasn't around. I was in my early 50s, I guess. We had moved to Port St. Williams from Harbour Devon just a couple of years before.

"Dad," said Dean. "A few months ago, a Bradley Browning contacted Deanna and me and asked to meet with us."

"What? That son-of-a-bitch," I said.

"So, you know him?" said Deanna.

"I know who he is," I said. "He tried to seduce your mother many years ago in St. John's. It is why we left St. John's after only one year and came back to Harbour Devon."

"Did he tell you he visited Harbour Devon to see mom about a year after you returned from St. John's?" asked Dean.

"Harbour Devon is small. I would have known," I said.

"He says you didn't know," said Deanna, almost crying.

"He says he was dropped off by a fisherman who brought him down from Port St. William," said Dean. "He had arranged to stay in the house of a friend who was away in St. John's for the summer. He says hardly anyone knew he was in town. He watched our house for several days and realized you went out fishing most mornings and didn't get back until the afternoon."

Deanna was sobbing by now. "Stop Dean. Can we just stop. We shouldn't do this."

"We have to, Deanna, for mom's sake. She is dying with guilt, and just wants dad to know so they can work it out somehow."

"Dean just tell me," I said.

"Dad, he visited mom while you were out fishing, and nine months later we were born. He says we are his children."

I sat down. Martha had never told me anything about this.

"What does mom say?" I asked.

Deanna jumped in. "She says she had sex with him in our house that morning while you weren't there. She says he left Harbour Devon shortly after that. She says he promised never to come back. She says it was the only time she was ever intimate with him, that she had not been with him that way when you and mom were in St. John's. She said he promised to stay out of your lives forever if she would just have sex with him. She has been guilty and grieving about it ever since. She says we could be his children, or we could be yours."

I was shocked, but I was far from innocent. I thought about my affair with Minnie.

Martha and I took years to work through the revelation that she had been unfaithful with Bradly Browning in our own house. I never told her about Minnie. Minnie was her best friend. It would have killed her. That was before DNA testing so there was no way to prove one way or the other who the father was. I didn't care much. Dean and Deanna were mine as far as I was concerned. I loved them as if they were mine. But I spent years looking at their facial features, their mannerisms, wondering, just wondering whether they were mine or that bastard, Bradley Browning's.

****

"But Uncle John, you said you were surprised when Bradley Browning told you many years later that he had an affair with Martha when you were in St. John's," Johnnie said.

"I was surprised because Martha swore the only time she was with him was in Harbour Devon when he came to visit. Perhaps she kept that from me for the same reason I kept my affair with Minnie from her. Perhaps we did it because we cared for each other. That's how I have to understand it."

****

Uncle John went home after he left Water Street that morning. Two hours later he walked to the florists and picked up two bunches of artificial flowers, the only kind that survived outdoors in the winter in Newfoundland. He walked back home, got a snow shovel out of his garage, threw it in the back of his truck, and drove to the cemetery on the far southern end of town.

He visited Martha's and Sarah's graves regularly; at least every couple of weeks. He kept flowers on their graves; live ones in the summer and artificial one in the winter. It had snowed several days before, so he knew he would have to clear the snow off their graves and headstones.

Sarah and Fred were buried side by side in a couple's plot. Martha and John had their couple's plot adjacent to them. Not by design, it just happened that way. Martha was buried in their plot and her name, date of birth and date of death engraved in the headstone. Above where Uncle John was to be buried, the headstone had his name and his birthdate, June 7, 1930, engraved. His date of death was yet to be known. John would lie in eternity between his two wives.

John arrived at the cemetery, picked up the two pots of artificial flowers off the passenger seat and grabbed the shovel from the back of the truck. He trudged through the snow to where the plots lay. John cleared away the snow, laid the two flower pots near the headstones of both his wives and stood back to look at them.

That will do, he thought. The flowers weren't real, but they provided some colour against the white snow. He stayed there for about 20 minutes, thinking about his wives, and talking to them in his mind. Then he turned and trudged back through the snow to his truck and drove home.

Chapter 7
Martha and Bradley

Bradley Browning had been watching the new girl all day. She had just been hired as a salesgirl in the women's clothing department of the Browning Department Store. He couldn't take his eyes off her. Her brown hair, angelic face, and slim body captivated him. Heir to the Browning fortune, Bradley, 30, was unmarried. He wasn't sure how old the young woman was or what her name was. His 55-year-old father still ran the store with a tight fist and took care of all the hiring—as well as the inventory, the front store, and managing the staff. Bradley had been educated in New York in business and management and his father had given him responsibility for the company's finances.

Bradley's office was in an elevated section of the store. It had a glass front and looked out over the women's clothing department. When he noticed the new girl was not with a customer and there was no one else around, he left his office, walked down the few steps to the main floor and strolled over to introduce himself.

"Hello," he said, offering his hand.

She shook his hand and said, "Are you lost? This is

the women's clothing department. But if this is where you want to be, can I help you?"

Very professional, Bradley noted. He smiled and said, "No, I'm not interested in buying any women's clothing. I'm here to introduce myself. I'm Bradley Browning, the business manager for the store."

Martha sputtered a bit and apologized for not recognizing him.

"That's OK," he said. "There's no reason why you would know who I am. I like to meet all the new employees. I need to meet with you to get some details for arranging your wages."

"I think I provided all the information to the department manager when I arrived this morning."

"There are a few other things, if you don't mind. Could you follow me up to my office? I will arrange for someone to cover this area for half an hour."

Bradley Browning turned, walked over to the desk and spoke with the department manager who nodded. He came back to where Martha was standing, and said, "Follow me please."

In the office overlooking the department store below, Bradley pulled the blind. "For privacy," he said.

"Oh, yes of course," said Martha.

"Please, have a seat," he said, indicating the chair by his desk. "So, Mrs. Parsons, Martha Parsons, I believe. You are married."

"Yes sir, my husband, John Parsons, and I married just last year in Harbour Devon and moved to St. John's a few months later. Looking for work and a new life."

"And what work has your husband found?"

"He is an elevator operator at Hotel Newfoundland. It's just for now until he can find something better. It doesn't pay well."

"I think it must not. I'm sure he will find something else. We have nothing for a man here right now ... You know we are a progressive business and hire married women. If you become pregnant though, and certainly after you have a child, we will have to lay you off. Company policy."

"Yes sir, I understand that."

"And what was your maiden name, Mrs. Parsons?"

"I was a White, sir."

"Oh, are you related to the Whites in Harbour Devon with the White's General Store and fish business?"

"Yes sir, my father owns that business. I worked in the store for years. Maybe it was that experience that got me this job. I don't know."

"I saw you engaging a customer earlier today and I was impressed. I wondered if you had experience in sales or the like."

"Thank you, sir. I do my best."

"Very well then Martha, may I call you Martha?"

"Yes sir, of course. That's my name. And I'm hardly used to Mrs. Parsons yet anyway."

"OK then, and please call me Bradley. Mr. Browning is my father." He smiled.

"Yes sir. Thank you, sir."

"My name isn't sir, either," he smiled.

Martha smiled back, feeling a little uncomfortable. A little too familiar, too soon. But he seems nice, she thought.

He set his hand on her shoulder as he opened the door for her. "Back to work now, Martha. I'm certain you will do well here."

****

It was a week before Bradley Browning approached Martha again, although he had been watching her every day and listening in on some of her interactions with customers and other staff.

He asked the manager of the women's clothing department if she thought Martha might be a good person to replace her when she left in a couple of months to have her baby. Her opinion was that Mrs. Parsons would do a good job as department manager, but she wondered to herself why he was overlooking some of the other women who had worked at Browning's longer. Bradley spoke with his father and a few days later called Martha into his office again.

"Martha, have a seat please," said Bradley, after pulling the curtains across his window.

Martha looked at him expectantly, not really sure what this call to the boss's office was all about. "Have I done something inappropriate, sir?"

"Not at all, Martha, my dear. Quite the opposite. We are happy with your work. I am trying to decide who to promote to women's clothing department manager. I have spoken with my father and we both agree we should offer you the position."

Somewhat shocked and feeling both honoured and a bit frightened, Martha said, "That is wonderful, sir. But I'm not certain what that would involve. My experience has always been in sales, not management."

"You underestimate yourself, Martha. And call me

Bradley, please. Mrs. Rawlins, the current section manager, knows the job well and she will fill you in. You'll learn quickly, I'm sure. You take over from her in two weeks—her pregnancy is starting to show. However, I do want to go over some of the details of the position with you myself. Perhaps you would agree to have lunch with me tomorrow when we can chat about it. There's a small restaurant across the street. How about I come down to the floor and we'll go over there at noon tomorrow?"

****

The next day at noon, Bradley came to the women's clothing department.

"Go gather your coat, Martha, I'll wait here."

"Yes sir, I mean yes Mr. … Bradley … I'll be back shortly."

Edna Rawlins looked at them as Martha walked away. "You be careful what you are up to, Mr. Browning, she's a married woman you know."

"What are you suggesting, Mrs. Rawlins?" Bradley smiled.

"You know very well what I am suggesting. It didn't work with me and it won't with her."

"We'll see Edna, we'll see. All I ask you to do is train

her well for the job she is about to take on."

"She'll be well trained. Don't you worry about that."

Martha came back with her coat on. Bradley placed his hand on her shoulder and guided her towards the door.

They chatted for an hour. About the store and her new job, but mostly about her and her life and then about his life as an only child and heir to the family business and family wealth. Martha sensed he was trying to impress her, and he did. His situation in St. John's was not unlike her position in Harbour Devon. She was also the only child in a family of some means, but on a smaller scale. They were alike in many ways. When they finished lunch and went back to the store, Martha felt like she and Bradley could be friends, could understand each other.

Martha loved John Parsons. She had chosen him over other potential suiters in Harbour Devon, but there was a connection with Bradley that she and John didn't have. But it was as a friend and colleague, not as a potential lover, she assured herself.

One of the things that Bradley had talked about was the annual trip to New York to choose clothing inventory – to learn what the fashions were to be for the coming year. He said the ladies of St. John's depended on them to have the latest fashions in their store, to keep up with London, New York, and Paris. He complimented Martha on how she dressed and said part of the job of the women's clothing department manager was to travel with the team to New York to choose the coming year's inventory. His father would be on the trip, as would he, and the other clothing department managers. It would be next month. He asked her if she would come along. All costs for her travel and accommodation would be covered, of course.

    Martha told John that evening after work all about her new job and about the request that she travel to New York with the purchasing team. She didn't mention the long lunch with Bradley Browning, that would come out many years later. John was excited and proud that she was making such an impression. He congratulated her and jokingly said his job continued to be the same—some ups, some downs.

****

    Martha had never flown before. It was frightening but she got through it. She was assigned a private room in their hotel in New York. The other two managers shared a room. The elder Mr. Browning and Bradley each had their own room.

The sales trip was busy. Many other groups from all over North America were attending the huge fashion show. For three days Martha helped the Brownings chose dresses and skirts and blouses and lingerie for the Browning Department Store.

On the first night everyone was so tired after the flight and the show that they all passed out in their rooms. On the second night, Mr. Browning had the whole group back to his suite for food and drinks and general discussion about the fashions. Halfway through the evening Bradley slipped a note into Martha's hand. It said, "Come to my room after, Room 501, I need to chat with you about something."

Martha was uncertain what to do. She went back to her room first. She freshened up, not admitting to herself why she felt the need to do that. She thought about John. Then she convinced herself that since Bradley was her boss and wanted to talk to her, she should go.

Bradley opened the door shortly after she knocked, "I'm glad you came, please come in." He was dressed in an expensive, dark blue, silk, robe which came down below his knees and was gathered around his abdomen with a tie."

"Why did you ask me to come, Bradley?"

"I so enjoyed our lunch and chat a couple of weeks

ago, I thought we could share a few drinks and chat some more."

"So it's not business, then," said Martha

"No, I guess it's not. Do you mind?" he said.

They were standing close together facing each other. He reached out and pulled her toward him, kissing her on the lips. She tightened at first and thought for a second about pulling away. But she didn't. She kissed him back.

****

A year after John and Martha went back to Harbour Devon, Martha wrote a letter to Bradley. She said she missed him and begged him to visit her in Harbour Devon. She said she wanted to leave John and go away with him to St. John's and restart the relationship they had.

Two months later Bradley showed up at her door. John was out fishing. Martha jumped in his arms as soon as the door closed behind him. Within 30 minutes they were in bed making love. As they lay in bed afterward, Bradley said, "Martha, there is something I have to tell you."

Martha got up on one elbow and looked at him, "What is that, my darling?" Those were the last words of endearment she would ever say to him.

Bradley told her he met another woman a few months after she left St. John's. They had fallen in love and were planning to marry within the year.

"Why did you do what you just did?" she asked, tears streaming down her face.

"I couldn't stop myself. There is still some feeling and you were so passionate."

"Get out," she said. "Leave now and never come back."

Two hours later John came in from fishing and found her crying.

"What's wrong sweetie?"

"Oh, just one of those days. Don't worry yourself. I'll be fine."

The next night they made love in the same bed she had shared with Bradley Browning.

Nine months later the twins were born.

***

Martha and John spent years talking through Martha's relationship with Bradley after Dean and Deanna made their revelation. Martha never did admit to her affair with Bradley Browning while they were in St. John's. She even implied that Bradley forced himself on her during his visit to Harbour Devon. John threatened to go to St. John's and confront him about it, but Martha talked him out if it, saying it was long ago and John might do something he ended up in prison for. She said Bradley had never really meant anything to her.

Chapter 8
Martha

Martha was born in 1933, daughter of the only merchant in Harbour Devon. She grew up privileged, compared to most other children in the town, although a merchant's daughter from St. John's might not have noticed a difference between Martha and the other Harbour Devon girls. Martha's dresses were just a bit prettier than the other girls, never homemade. Usually bought by her father in St. John's when he travelled to order merchandise for his general store. Her father's money came from the sales in the store and also from fishing. He owned a schooner and not only fished himself but bought dried fish from other fishermen. He sold the fish to the larger companies in St. John's who shipped salt cod to Portugal and other countries in Europe.

It might be difficult to understand why Martha married John Parsons. Sometimes Martha didn't quite understand herself. She wondered many times whether she had made the right choice. There had been opportunities before and during their marriage, for her to go in a different direction. It wasn't until the last two years of their life together that she knew, with all certainly, that she had made the right choice. She was thankful that John had never left her during their bumpy life together.

During her teenage years, she was interested in Paul Kennedy from Dorset Cove. There were no cars in those days, and no roads to drive on if there were. Dorset Cove was a 30-minute walk along a gravel trail from Harbour Devon. A Sunday outing was to walk to Dorset Cove from Harbour Devon, often meeting people from that community coming the other way. The school and the church and the stores were all in Harbour Devon so people from Dorset Cove had reason to go there. The reverse was not always true—although Martha had a reason. She knew that she and the other girls would meet the boys from Dorset Cove coming in the other direction. Martha was interested in one of those boys. She really liked Paul Kennedy. The problem was Paul liked Minnie Carter, and Minnie was almost always with him on his walk to Harbour Devon.

But one Sunday she was not. Martha, generally polite and not one to barge in, saw her chance. Instead of passing by and saying hello to the boys, as usual, Martha stopped.

"Hello, Paul," said Martha.

Paul was startled. He looked towards who had said his name. It was Martha White, the merchant's daughter. He knew Martha from school, as an acquaintance, nothing more. She was three years younger than him. Paul's good friend, John Parsons, had a thing for her but he never could get up enough courage to approach her and say anything more than "Hello."

"Hello, Martha," said Paul. "How ya doin' today?"

Martha drew up every bit of courage she could muster, went over, took him by the arm, and said, "I'm fine, Paul. Can I walk with you?"

The phrase *Can I walk with you?* was loaded. Everybody knew it meant, "I like you. I'm interested in you." That sort of thing.

Paul was startled. He looked around to make sure Minnie hadn't decided to come after all, then looked down at Martha's arm, tucked into his. "Sure."

The other guys and girls walked on and left them.

"Lovely Sunday for a walk, isn't it?" said Martha.

"It is indeed," said Paul.

Later they sat on a rock, the warm July sun shining on their faces, talking about school which would start up again in a couple of months, about what they were doing that summer, and about a dance in the parish hall in two weeks' time. Martha reached over and held Paul's hand. "Would you like to take me to that dance, Paul?"

Paul knew Minnie would be expecting him to take her to the dance. Martha knew that too. He really liked Minnie. They were courting. Martha was butting in. Martha was the merchant's daughter, which carried a lot of prestige. But he didn't want to hurt Minnie. Minnie's father was a fisherman. They weren't well off. Paul's father was a teacher in Harbour Devon. His mother worked in the White's general store. If he said no to Minnie, would it affect his mother's job? He didn't think so. He decided then and there.

"I've already asked Minnie," he said.

"Oh, that's too bad," said Martha, letting go of his hand. "Would have been a lot of fun, you and me, I mean. I guess I'll have to see if John Parsons will go with me." She smiled, knowing that Paul and John were good friends, and he would probably mention it to John, and then John might get up the nerve to ask her. Maybe Paul would get jealous if she went with John. And John Parsons and Minnie Carter would be a better pair anyway, she thought. Maybe she could get them to hook up. Then she and Paul might have a chance. They would make a better pair than Minnie and Paul, she thought.

Two weeks later Paul and Minnie, and John and Martha, went to the summer dance.

In 1959, the two couples married.

Many years later, the two couples, married with teenaged children, were still good friends. Martha watched as John and Minnie became very friendly. It started with the shared vacation on their boats in 1977. She was pretty certain they remained *very* friendly until she and John moved to Port St. William.

Frankly, Martha didn't pay a lot of heed to John and Minnie and the affair she thought they might be having because she and Paul had also reconnected in 1977. Not reconnecting from that short encounter on the road to Dorset Cove when they were teens, but reconnecting from an encounter in 1961, just after Bradley Browning came to visit and left Martha in an emotional crisis. She couldn't go to John for support, he would have been devastated if he had known what had really been going on between her and Bradley. So she turned to someone else – Paul. For a few months they were intimate until Martha realized she was pregnant. Then they broke it off. Martha always hoped it might be Paul she was pregnant by, but the twins that resulted look too much like John for that to be the case. But she always wondered. She had had sex with three men and the timing was such that either of them could be the father of her children. Just thinking that made Martha feel terrible. Was she really that kind of woman?

The affair between Paul and Martha happened as John and Minnie were doing the same thing. The couples didn't see each other much after John and Martha moved to Port St. William. The two communities were in the same bay but far enough apart that a trip from one to the other did not happen without planning.

Martha was 47 when she and John moved to Port St. William. John gave up fishing and began working with the Department of Fisheries. Two years later Dean and Deanna reported on their meeting with Bradley Browning and his claim that he may be their father.

For two more years, she and John fought and talked and argued and cried. But they stuck together. Martha confessed to having had sex with Bradley when he came to Port St. William to see her. She never mentioned the letter she had sent to him asking if he would come and rescue her from her miserable life. She never mentioned the intimate affair she and Bradley had in St. John's. And neither she nor

John admitted to the affairs the other had had with their best friends, Paul and Minnie.

But John did shock her when he confessed about his time with Sarah Hawkins. Sarah was Martha's first cousin. Fred and Sarah Hawkins had always been good friends of John and Martha. Until they moved to Port St. William, John and Martha always stayed at Fred and Sarah's house when they visited the town. The affair had been in the late 1960s and lasted for a year or so. Martha realized that Sarah was to John what Paul was to her, a childhood attraction that never went away. Martha found it difficult, but eventually she and John worked through it all—or as much as they would admit. John never knew about Paul and her, and Martha, at least officially, did not know about John and Minnie.

Martha was diagnosed with breast cancer in 1992. After a three-year battle, she died in her own home, being nursed and loved and cared for by the man she had chosen and, in the end, the one she had stayed with.

Chapter 9
Dean and Deanna

The twins had different birthdays and were born in different years: Dean at 11:51 p.m. on December 31, 1962 and Deanna at 12:05 a.m. on January 1, 1963.

They were best friends and like two peas in a pod until about age 10. Then, during those in-between years from age 11 to 15, they grew into individuals. Dean was interested in girls, hockey, and fly fishing, Deanna read books, spent far too much time in her room, and didn't seem to be able to sort out who she was. Dean and Deanna remained friends but were not close like they once were. They tolerated each other, generally got along, and didn't outright fight all that much. Probably a result of being in different worlds most of the time. Their parents weren't really strict, and as long as the twins didn't seem to be heading towards a life of crime and seemed to be coping and doing well in school, they pretty much left them alone.

Dean and Deanna were teenagers in the 1970s. The age of disco. Going to school dances was important and by then, even in the outports, rock and roll and disco had replaced square dances. The word *time*—as nighttime social gatherings with dancing had long been called—was replaced simply by the word *dance*. This change in tradition was initiated to a large degree by the kids who were coming home from Memorial University, where modern dancing and other activities, including doing drugs, was ahead of the outports—if one could say that rock and roll and drugs was "ahead" of the traditional square dance and alcohol. Not that alcohol wasn't used in abundance by kids going to university. And they *were* kids.

High school finished after grade 11 and most students were still just 17 years old when they started university. Barely old enough to have a driver's licence, not old enough to drink alcohol legally, full of hormones, and chomping at the bit to get away from parents so they could try out the free side of life. That's how old Dean and Deanna were in 1979 when they headed off to Memorial University. Dean's interest was in business and Deanna thought she wanted to become a teacher. That's not where either of them ended up.

****

"Deanna, wanna come with us? We're heading over to the Breezeway," said Joanne, Deanna's roommate.

Joanne stood by the open door to their room. Their

friend Ruth Jackman, looking in, said, "Sure come on b'y, can't spend all your time with your head in the books."

Deanna considered it for a second, but she was happy where she was. "Naw, I think I'll stay here and finish this book. Then I got a paper I have to get finished up."

"Well, suit yourself, but if you change your mind, we're at the Breezeway."

Deanna switched from education to political science. A woman with strong feminist views, within five years of finishing her degree, Deanna got married, had a son, and got divorced. Her husband couldn't deal with a strong woman, is how Deanna explained her failed marriage. Being very active in women's rights and domestic violence issues, Deanna was nominated for, and served on, the Provincial Advisory Council on the Status of Women. Later she was on the Canadian version of the same council.

Eventually, Deanna went back to Memorial and studied social work. She worked in that field for the rest of her career. She never remarried. Her son got heavily into drugs. Most of the time she didn't know where he was. Most of the time Deanna was sad.

****

Dean quit commerce after two years at Memorial and went into science. He ended with a physics degree. Loved it but couldn't make a living at it. After getting a degree at Memorial, he went to the College of the North Atlantic and trained to be an electrician. He completed the coursework in half the time most people take because of the credits he got for his physics degree.

The other thing Dean did during his seven years in St. John's was fall in love with Betty Dawe. She got pregnant, they got married, and had a daughter, Norah. Norah was born in 1984, and a year later, Betty and Dean headed back to Harbour Devon, and then on to Port St. William where Dean established himself as the only fully qualified electrician in town. Betty, a true-blue townie, took to the outport life like a fish to water. They had three more children.

****

Norah Parsons, at age 12, ran away from home. Norah said afterwards that she felt her parents didn't understand her and were keeping her from doing what she wanted to do.

"Keeping you from what you want to do," said her mother, Betty, in frustration. "Well, what is it you want to do?"

"I want to go out with my friends at night. I have to be in by 7 o'clock. They can stay out until 10."

"But Norah, sweetie," Dean said, "you're in school, you have homework. You need your sleep so you can function in school the next day. You can't be outdoors all night."

"You see, that's what I mean. You don't understand. I'll never get a boyfriend if I have to be in the house all the time."

"Boyfriend. Boyfriend!" said her mother. "You're too young for a boyfriend."

"No, I'm not. My friends have boyfriends."

"Who? Does Wanda have a boyfriend? Or Sandra. They're your best friends, aren't they?"

"No, they don't have boyfriends. But they're tied down by their parents. Just like me."

"So, who are we talking about?" asked her mother.

"You know, Mary Saunders and Tanya Pike, and girls like that."

Dean broke in. "They're 15-year-olds, sweetie.

They're older than you. Not that 15 is old enough to be out all night. They should be in doing homework long before 10 p.m., just like you."

"But they're not and the boys like them."

"OK," said Dean, looking at Betty. "Let's say that one night a week you can stay out until 8."

"No, 10," said Norah.

"No, not 10, but 9 p.m. OK?" said her mother.

"Which night," asked Norah, thinking she was finally starting to get somewhere.

"Which night would you like?" asked her father.

"Wednesday," said Norah.

"How about Friday," said Betty.

"I can already stay out until 8 p.m. on Friday and Saturdays. That's only one hour different."

"I tell you what we'll do. We'll let you stay out until 9 p.m. every Friday and Saturday night, but all other nights you have to be in by 7:30 p.m. That's half an hour more every night when you have school the next day. But you must get your homework done after school. It has to be done before you go out after supper."

Norah took it. She knew she had made some progress and wouldn't push any more for now. "OK, that's good. Or at least better." But for Norah it was just the thin edge of the wedge. She would keep pushing.

By 14, Norah had a boyfriend. Which in itself wasn't unusual, but he was 16, a school drop-out, and known to do drugs. And the more Dean and Betty found out about him the worse it got. They told Norah he was too old for her.

Norah got pregnant when she was 15, and in 1999 had a baby girl. The father, Wildred Snow, left Port St. William and was never seen in the area again. Norah named her baby girl Charlotte. They lived with Dean and Betty Parsons who raised them both. They were both children really.

Chapter 10
On The Wharf
Saturday, May 4, 2019

Sunrise was complete. A gap of sky was just visible between the ocean and the bottom of the sun.

"That was a nice one," said Johnnie.

"It was," said Uncle John.

"I got a job with the town council, working on the roads for the summer," said Johnnie.

"That's great. Got to help pay for your university costs. How was your first year at university, by the way?"

"Pretty good. I'm doing well. Just general studies. Got all As. I think I'll apply to engineering for next year."

"Inclined that way, are you?" said Uncle John.

"I think so."

"You must be 19 now are you, Johnnie?"

"Will be soon, May 28. You'll be 89 in June, right? My God, Uncle John, they're going to have to shoot you on judgement day."

"Yes, I suppose. I've heard that saying applied to old people before. People who you think will never die. But I'll die, just like everyone else. Of course, you never know when, and at my age, you know there is a strong likelihood it will be sooner rather than later."

"I just can't imagine life without you being around, and without our Saturday morning meetings on the wharf."

"It will all end, and life will go on without me being around."

"Yes, I suppose, one day. But see if you can hang around for a while, OK?"

"OK," Uncle John smiled.

Silence fell as they both contemplated life. Then Uncle John said, "I understand you and Charlotte, my great-granddaughter, are going out, or dating, or seeing each other, whatever you call it these days."

"Yes, we've been going out on and off since late high school really. It was a bit rocky for the first term at university, but we had a couple of dates in second term. We are sort of an item again now. I like her. I think she likes me."

"I see. She isn't back from St. John's yet. Got a job in town I understand."

"Yes, that's true. I'm going into town on the May 24th weekend to see her."

"OK, so it is serious, then?"

"Well, maybe. As I said, we get along really well."

"Be careful."

"What?"

"You know. Wear condoms and stuff like that."

"Jeez, Uncle John, you're embarrassing me."

"Why? Am I not right in assuming you're having sex?"

"Well, yes, but, Uncle John, you're her great-grandfather for God's sake."

"And I was 19 once, too."

"OK, can we talk about something else?"

"Sure."

"Uncle John, remember the talk we had about your wife Martha, and that Browning guy, and you not knowing if Dean, Charlotte's grandfather, was really your son?"

"Yes, I remember."

"So, it is possible I am not going out with your great-granddaughter, isn't it?"

"No, she's my great-granddaughter. I didn't tell you, but we had genetic testing done a couple of years after Bradley Browning showed up back in 2005. Dean and Deanna are mine."

"Oh, that's great. So, I will be related to you by

marriage … if Charlotte and I were to marry, I mean."

"Big 'if' seeing as you are just starting your relationship, wouldn't you think?"

"We really like each other, Uncle John."

"Johnnie, this relationship with my great-granddaughter seems to be getting more serious by the minute."

"Is it a problem?"

"No, I suppose not. Just don't get into a serious relationship unless you mean it and know what you're doing."

"You sound like my father."

"Or perhaps more like your grandfather," Uncle John smiled.

"Yes, I guess."

"Sometimes it feels like you are my grandfather, the way we talk. I wish you were my grandfather, Uncle John."

"You didn't know your grandfather, Fred Hawkins, did you Johnnie? He treated your grandmother well—when he was around anyway. I'm just a substitute, and because I married your grandmother after your grandfather died, it seems appropriate, I guess."

"Yah, I never knew Pop Hawkins. I was born two

years after he died."

"Yes, that's right you were," said Uncle John. "There's a lot more to his story. I'll tell you sometime, when the time is right."

"Now you got me curious, Uncle John."

"Yes, I suppose. Well don't worry yourself about it. But you keep me up-to-date about how things are going with you and my great-granddaughter."

"Will do. See you next Saturday, Uncle John"

Chapter 11
On The Wharf
Saturday, August 21, 2021

"Summer will soon be over," said Johnnie.

"It will," said Uncle John.

Uncle John and Johnnie had arrived on the wharf a little early. The morning birds were chirping. The sun was still below the horizon, maybe 15 minutes from suddenly popping out of the water with its first true ray of light. Before that moment, diffuse light of red, orange, and yellow would be lighting up the morning sky. But it wouldn't be until the tip of the sun popped up out of the water that sunrise would truly start.

"We can't see it, but we know it's there. We know it's coming," said Johnnie.

"Yes, we know," said Uncle John. "We have faith."

Johnnie looked at Uncle John. "You're familiar with that quote, aren't you? The one by the Indian poet. I heard it first this past year."

"Faith is the bird that feels the light and sings when the dawn is still dark," said Uncle John.

"Yes, that one. I guess it means that sometimes, even

when we can't see something or don't know for sure, we know in our hearts that something 'is' or that something will happen."

"We know, we have faith that the sun will rise this morning like every morning," said Uncle John.

"Unless the apocalypse happens," said Johnnie.

"There is that," said Uncle John.

The sun's rays shouted at them as it rose out of the water.

"No apocalypse today," said Johnnie. "The bird was right to have faith."

"You are gaining wisdom, Johnnie."

"Maybe university is good for something after all."

"You gain knowledge in university, Johnnie. Not wisdom," said Uncle John.

"So where do you think wisdom comes from, Uncle John? You seem to have a bunch of it," said Johnnie.

"Time, experience, making bad choices, making good choices, being wrong, being right, and learning from all that life throws at you. And perhaps being educated formally helps too. Hopefully that way you'll eventually be wiser than me. Which shouldn't be too hard. I made all the mistakes early on, but unfortunately the wisdom I gained from them came too late to stop the consequences."

"Flying into windows, are you," Johnnie laughed, recalling Uncle John's comment years earlier.

"Something like that. It's unfortunate though when one person's past actions come back, not to affect them, but someone else."

"What do you mean?" asked Johnnie. "Is there a story coming?"

"Johnnie, you and Charlotte are finishing university after this coming year. Charlotte will get a teaching job and I know you already have a good shot at a job with AP Construction in St. John's. And then I guess it's marriage."

"We are talking about getting married in a few years, maybe August 2024. We want you at the wedding, so hang around, will you?"

"Johnnie, you asked if there was a story coming and there is. And it affects you. Nobody else alive knows what I am about to tell you, and you are never to mention it to anyone except Charlotte. In fact, you and Charlotte have to talk about it and make a decision."

****

Sarah White and I were born on the same day in

1930. My mother suffered the pain of childbirth in her home in Harbour Devon and Sarah's mother went through it in Port St. William. We wouldn't know this until years later when we met as children. The Parsons and Whites had become friends. My father and Mr. White met during the seal hunt.

Travel between the two communities was by boat back then, and if there was an overnight stay needed, we would accommodate each other. It was 1938, the war in Europe hadn't started yet, and we Parsons had made a visit to Port St. William. I think it was to buy Christmas gifts or something—my parents always felt the prices were better in Port St. William for Christmas shopping. Probably a grass-is-always-greener situation. I'm sure the shopping was limited anyway, because cash and availability of merchandise to buy were limited. Sarah and I met for the first time that year.

"Bet you can't catch me," I said, as I ran out the door and up over the hill that rose out of the ground in back of the White's house.

Sarah, who was right behind me, said, "Oh yes I can." And a few seconds later she was flying past me. She was always more fit and physically capable then me.

We both managed to get up over the steep hill and fell on the yellowing grass, panting and laughing. Lying on our backs we squinted at the bright sun. A late autumn chill hung in the air but no snow yet. A few minutes later the Whites' dog, Spot, came running up the hill, jumping all over us and licking our faces.

It's funny how you remember moments like that. I don't recall much more about that visit or other visits to the Whites' house in Port St. William during my childhood.

The next time I recall meeting Sarah was 10 years later, around 1948, after the war. We were both in Grade 11, in different schools. Both Port St. William and Harbour Devon were big enough, with about 1000 people each, to have schools that went from Grade 1 to 11. Port St. William would eventually grow to be the bigger place, with abut 2000 residents by the 1960s.

In 1948, the Harbour Devon High School boys' soccer team were on a trip to Port St. William to play the local soccer team. That was a rarity back then. There weren't many sports games between schools in the outports. But both schools had teachers who were avid soccer fans.

Sarah ran over to me and gave me a hug when she saw me on the Harbour Devon side of the field before the game started. "I'm cheering for our team, but I thought I'd give you a big welcome hug anyway," she said with a smile.

"It's great to see you again."

"Eh, Sarah, come on back over here and leave that Harbour Devon guy alone," a boy from the other side called out to her.

"Gotta go. It's my boyfriend, Fred Hawkins," she said. Then she came close and whispered in my ear. "But I think I'm ready for a change."

We lost the game, but I won with Sarah. Her boyfriend went off to celebrate their win with the boys. Sarah and I held hands and kissed outside her father's stage in the moonlight. Another moment I remember well.

In 1962, Sarah married her boyfriend of 14 years, Fred Hawkins. In 1968, nine years after Martha and I married, I met up with Sarah again. She was still living in Port St. William. Fred was working on the lake boats, as he had for years. He spent three months away on the Great Lakes and then would come home for a month. By 1968 there was a road between Harbour Devon and Port St. William, and I had a car. I was a fisherman and had reason to go to Port St. William periodically because they had a good marine supplies store where I could get boating and fishing supplies. During one of those visits I ran into Sarah. We got talking and remembering the old days, and one thing led to another. A few months later, on one of our encounters in Port St. William, we slept together. In her house in the daytime when her kids were in school. Fred was away on the lake boats. For over a year it continued. I went to Port St. William every chance I got. Then one day Sarah grabbed me as I came through the door to her house. and said, "John, I'm pregnant. I'm two weeks past my period. I feel pregnant. I know what it feels like. Fred has been away for almost three months. It's yours, John."

"Yes, I know, my love," I said. We had been expressing our love to each other by then. We had talked about the possibility of leaving our spouses and somehow getting together. But we knew it was not possible. We had children to consider. And now this would force the issue.

"We have to stop, John. We have to give it all up. Fred is back in two weeks. We'll have sex that first night he's back. When the baby comes, I'll say it was early. No one will suspect. But we must stop now, John."

We made love for the last time that day. I never came back to visit. The baby boy was born vigorous and healthy. They called him Spencer—your father, Johnnie. I'm your grandfather. Fred never knew or suspected, as far as I know. Thirty years later I married your grandmother, as you know."

"Wait, wait, Uncle John. Stop talking. You are my grandfather? Like for real?"

"Yeah, for real, Johnnie."

"Well that's great, isn't it? I never knew Pop Hawkins, anyway, so I don't feel upset. You've been like a grandfather to me anyway."

"You're not thinking, Johnnie. I am also Charlotte's great-grandfather."

Johnnie was silent. Then he realized what it might mean. "Are we too close?"

"I don't know, Johnnie. I think it's OK. There are lots of other genes in the mix – Hawkins, and Greens, and Snows, and Dawes. But I don't know. You're sort of like third cousins, you and Charlotte, but closer because it's not me on one side and my brother on the other, it is me on both sides. I've given it a lot of thought. I'm pretty sure its legal, and the church would also be OK with it. I just don't know if it would cause trouble with your children."

"Jesus, Uncle John. I have to talk to Charlotte."

"Yes, you do. But try to convince her not to speak with anybody else about it. Although perhaps you two should talk to a doctor in St. John's when you go back."

"Yes, that's what we'll do. Yes, we'll do that."

Not much else was said as they walked off the wharf that morning. Johnnie was deep in thought.

****

Uncle John went home, got in his truck, and drove to the cemetery. Not to visit his two wives, he had done that just two days before. This time he went there to talk to Fred Hawkins, to look him in the eye, so to speak, and ask him again what he had asked him many years ago.

Fred Hawkins continued his pattern of three months in Ontario followed by one month in Port St. William for his whole working life, right up to a few years before he died, when he moved home permanently. When Fred had visited him in prison, Uncle John had made him swear he would give up his double life and commit to Sarah. Uncle John had always believed Fred had done that, but today, relating his story about Sarah and him to Johnnie, had made Uncle John wonder whether Fred had really parted ways with Chen Wong.

Uncle John stood at the foot of Fred Hawkins' grave and stared at his headstone. There was nothing, of course. No voice from the heavens, no sounds from under the ground, and Uncle John didn't expect there would be. He just wondered if by coming here and being near to Fred, he could get closer to the truth. Perhaps he could get back to that time after Fred and Sarah's wedding when he asked Fred bluntly if he had entirely broken off with Chen and truly committed to Sarah. At the time, Fred had responded with indignation and swore his love and his life were with Sarah. Uncle John had believed him then and wasn't sure why now, decades later, he began to doubt. He stood over Fred's grave for a long time. Hearing Fred's words from the past and trying to fit them with the doubts he felt today. He would never know, he decided, and should just put it all behind him.

Uncle John got in his truck and drove home.

Chapter 12
Johnnie and Charlotte

Charlotte couldn't remember her great-grandmother, because Martha Parsons died five years before she was born. But her great-grandfather, John Parsons, Uncle John—Old Pop to her—was still alive. Norah Parsons had given birth to Charlotte when she was just 15 years old. Charlotte never knew her father, he left when her mom became pregnant with her and never came back. Her mother's parents, Dean and Betty Parsons, or Young Pop and Nan as Charlotte knew them, helped a lot. As far as Charlotte was concerned, she had three parents.

Charlotte and Johnnie both grew up in Port St. William, so they had known each other all their lives. They started Kindergarten the same year. They moved through school year by year. Always in the same class. At first, he was just one of the stupid boys to her, and she was just one of the silly girls to him. Then one year something happened – hormones. It happened to Charlotte first and she became attracted to the older boys who were filling out, but then Johnnie started to change, and he started to look attractive to her as well. Johnnie didn't show much interest in her at first.

He went out with a few other girls for a while. When Charlotte and Johnnie were 17, they were at a teenage dance and Johnnie asked her to dance. She decided to accept his offer because the guy she was interested in wasn't paying her any attention. Maybe dancing with Johnnie would make him jealous, she thought. But something different happened. Johnnie talked to her while they were dancing, rather than breathing on her neck and trying to nibble her ears. He held her hand after the dance and she decided not to pull away. It went from there. They started hanging around together and by the time they both went to university the next year they were an item—high school sweethearts leaving their small town and heading off to the big city. They had sex for the first time that first year away from home.

 The job Charlotte had in St. John's the summer between first and second year university finished in mid-August, so she only had a couple of weeks at home before going back to school. Johnnie worked with the town council in Port St. William from May to the end of August, so they were apart most of the summer. When she was home that summer, Charlotte went to visit Old Pop one day and Johnnie went along.

 "Morning Charlotte. Mornin' Johnnie."

"Morning Old Pop," said Charlotte.

"Morning, Uncle John," said Johnnie. "Great sunrise this morning wasn't it?"

"It was that," said Uncle John.

"Right, I forgot. You guys watch the sun rise every Saturday morning," said Charlotte.

"You should join us next week, Charlotte," suggested Johnnie with some enthusiasm although he immediately wished he hadn't suggested it. The sunrise was for him and Uncle John. But he didn't have to worry.

"I think I'll pass on that," said Charlotte. "I like my bed too much."

"Would you like a cup of tea?" asked Uncle John.

"Sure," they said in unison.

Uncle John put the kettle on. He had lived alone since Sarah died nine years previous. Uncle John could be seen walking around Port St. William most days. He had regular walking routes and most people knew where he would be on his journey around town at any time of day. He always had lunch at a small café that was started up about 15 years before. Always had ham and cheese on a croissant, a cup of Earl Grey tea, and a glass of water. It was ready for him as he walked through the door every day at 12:30 p.m.

When the Earl Grey tea was steeped to his liking, Uncle John poured it into three teacups and brought them on a tray with the teapot and a few biscuits. He bought the biscuits and his other groceries regularly every week from Coleman's grocery store.

"Thanks, Old Pop," said Charlotte.

"You're welcome, my sweetie," said Uncle John. "You're one of the few of my many descendants who comes to visit these days. Least I can do is serve you tea and biscuits." He smiled.

"Perhaps I should start calling you Old Pop," said Johnnie with a smirk on his face.

"Uncle John is fine. I've got enough people calling me 'old.'"

"Do you mind?" asked Charlotte.

"Mind what, sweetie?"

"Being called Old Pop," said Charlotte.

"Naw," said Uncle John. "Then my son couldn't be called Young Pop, and you know how much he likes that."

They laughed and sipped, nibbled, and chatted. Charlotte and Johnnie left. Uncle John hadn't said anything, but he was worried. Just what would it mean if they eventually got married and had children?

****

Over the next couple of years in university Johnnie and Charlotte had a rough time with their relationship. They fought, Charlotte broke it off for a while and went out with another guy for a couple of months. They got back together.

Then in the summer of 2021, before the beginning of their last year in university, when Johnnie was about to finish his engineering degree and Charlotte her teaching degree, Uncle John dropped his bombshell. Johnnie thought for sure that Uncle John's revelation that he was Johnnie's grandfather would be Charlotte's reason for ending their relationship. But instead it hardened her resolve to make their relationship work.

"Everything I read tells me we're OK," she said to Johnnie one night. They were living together in St. John's in a small apartment they had rented at the beginning of their last year at Memorial. Johnnie bought a ring, they got engaged, and set August 19, 2024 as their wedding date. Still over two years away but it gave them time to settle into their jobs and plan the wedding.

"What do you mean?" said Johnnie.

"This thing about us being related. The consanguinity thing, I believe is the word. I figure we are either second or third cousins. It's not like both of us having the same great-grandfather, which would make us third cousins, my great-grandfather is your grandfather. We are sort of like second-and-a-half cousins. And with true third cousins both the great-grandfather and great-grandmother are the same but, in our case, it is only the great-grandfather that is the same. Anyway, best as I can sort out, there is very little reason to worry. I don't think we are at more risk of having children with genetic problems than the general population. But I also think we should talk to a geneticist."

"OK," said Johnnie. "How do we arrange that?"

"Go see our family doctor and get her to refer us, I guess."

That's what they did, and the geneticist confirmed Charlotte's research. They probably didn't need to worry.

Time went quickly. A few months after the wedding Charlotte was pregnant and in August 2025, little Jason was born.

****

Johnnie and Charlotte's relationship had had rocky times over the previous five years but nothing like after Jason's birth. He seemed fine at first. He was a little slow to cry but then screamed and changed from sort of blue to a nice pink colour. But things weren't so good after they went home. At first, Johnnie and Charlotte thought it was just because they were new parents and didn't know what newborns were supposed to be like. Jason always seemed to be short of breath and his breathing was noisy; he wasn't growing well. Charlotte worried he wasn't getting enough milk. She started supplementing her breast feeding. He hardly took the bottle at all. His grandparents, Mary and Spencer Hawkins, came to visit them in St. John's about three weeks after Jason's birth. Mary was worried. What she was seeing did not seem normal at all.

Neither Mary nor Spencer knew that Spencer was Uncle John's son. Johnnie and Charlotte had been true to their promise to Uncle John to never to tell anyone. As far as Johnnie and Charlotte were concerned, Fred and Sarah Hawkins were Spencer's parents. That is what Spencer knew, that is how he grew up and there was no reason to change that. Uncle John agreed with them.

Mary insisted they take the child to a doctor. Within hours Jason was admitted to Pediatric Intensive Care at the Janeway Children's Hospital. Jason had heart failure. They were told he had several heart defects that would require medication and eventually surgery.

It was a long downhill path. Jason was transferred to the SickKids in Toronto and then to the Children's Hospital of Eastern Ontario where he had heart surgery. He died a few months after surgery.

It had all been too stressful. Charlotte blamed the heart defects on consanguinity. She told Spencer what she knew. He was furious and went to see Uncle John. Uncle John was alone in his house when Spencer arrived.

****

Spencer knocked on the door. It took 95-year-old Uncle John a while to get to the door and open it. Spencer pushed the door open and barged in, knocking Uncle John over.

"Get your ass off the floor old man, we have to talk," said Spencer as he reached out his hand to help Uncle John get up on his feet.

"How did you find out?" asked Uncle John.

"Charlotte told me. She is pissed at you and blames you for Jason's death."

"She's probably right," said Uncle John as he sat on his sofa. Spencer was in the chair across the coffee table from him.

"Why the fuck did you never tell me about this? Why did mom never tell me?" said Spencer.

"It didn't matter before. It only matters now because of Johnnie and Charlotte."

"I spent my life thinking Fred Hawkins was my father."

"He was your father. He loved you, he raised you. He was your mother's husband."

"You're bloody right he was my father. A better father than you could ever have been. I never knew what my mother ever saw in you. Never understood why she married you. Even now, knowing what I know, I don't understand."

"We were in love in those younger days, Spencer. We truly were."

"It doesn't matter, you had no right having an affair with another man's wife. You betrayed your own wife. You betrayed your friend. Because Fred Hawkins was your friend, wasn't he? From all I've heard you say he was."

"He was. And I am so sorry. Not sorry for loving your mother, but sorry for acting on how I felt. I betrayed everyone. We both did. But when your mother got pregnant with you, we decided it was best to let go. To never be together again. To never let anyone know. It would cause too much hurt. When your father died, we got together just to have each other. We swore we would never tell. If it hadn't been for my grandson and my great-granddaughter falling in love, I would have gone to my grave with this knowledge."

"When did you tell them? Did you tell them in time for them to decide not to marry?"

"Yes, I told them three years before they got married. They studied all about it and even saw a geneticist. The conclusion was that the risk was low. But low is not zero. Little Jason showed us that."

"What a fuckup, John. What a mess. Johnnie and Charlotte are fighting and crying all the time. I don't think their marriage can survive this. All because of what you and mom did. You should never have done it, John. I don't understand why."

"Do you love Mary, Spencer?" said Uncle John.

"Of course, I do," said Spencer.

"Would you ever hurt her? Would you ever cheat on her?"

Spencer paused. He wondered if Uncle John knew about the troubles he and Mary had about 10 years before. He wondered if Johnnie mentioned it during the many chats he and Uncle John had on the wharf every Saturday. "I have not always been a perfect husband, but I have never done anything that got us in the mess you got us in."

Uncle John looked at Spencer. "So what do we do now? Do we let the world know or do we put it back in the box that your mother and I had it in?"

"I know and accept you are my biological father and Spencer is your grandson. But the way I remember my life and my real father will not change. Because Fred Hawkins is my real father as far as I am concerned. So yes, let's put it back in the box."

"You should talk to Johnnie and Charlotte about doing the same thing."

"I will John. Goodbye. Try to stay away from me as much as you can."

Spencer left and closed the door a little bit too loud behind him.

****

"I want a divorce, Johnnie."

Johnnie did, too. They had been fighting for months. By the end of 2027 the divorce was finalized. The little they had was split between them.

Chapter 13
On The Wharf
Saturday, July 15, 2028

"The sunrise was good this morning, grandfather," said Johnnie, as he brought his cellphone up close to Uncle John's face so he could see the picture he had taken.

"Yes, I can see," said Uncle John, squinting.

"How are things with you, grandfather?"

"Being 98 is no fun, Johnnie. I can't get down to the wharf with you anymore, somebody gets my groceries for me, most of my meals are brought to me, I don't think they trust me around the stove. If it wasn't for the fact that I can still look after myself in the bathroom and get myself dressed with my shoes on the right feet most days, I would probably be in a home."

"Your mind is still good though."

"Well I guess I have to depend on you and the rest of the family to tell me that. Because how would I know if I was talking garbage?"

"Well you're not talking garbage any more than you always did." Johnnie smiled. "That was a joke, Uncle John."

"You called me Uncle John. You forget sometimes

that you call me grandfather now."

"No, it was a test. To see if you noticed."

"Now *you're* talking garbage." Uncle John smiled.

"You're still quick, grandfather."

"So how long are you back home in Port St. William this time? I know you've been through a rough couple of years with the baby and the divorce. You still got your job in St. John's?"

"Yeah, my job at AP Construction is good. I met someone. She's from St. John's with no connection to back this way. At least none that I know about. Her name is Penny Warren."

The name meant nothing to Uncle John. This time, he thought, my past won't come back to hurt people.

"Well, I'm on my way now grandfather," said Johnnie. "I'm driving back to St. John's tomorrow so I'm back for work on Monday. See you again when I'm back. Maybe I'll have Penny with me next time. Introduce her to the family and all."

Chapter 14
Penny Warren

There was no one quite like Penelope Chen Warren. At least not in Johnnie's opinion. Like Johnnie, she was an engineer. Penny started work at AP Construction a few years after Johnnie had. She started in the fall, just a few months before Johnnie's divorce was finalized.

Penny was 24 years old when Johnnie met her, but to Johnnie her life story was longer than that. Penny's parents were both teachers. They had finished their training at Memorial University around the turn of the century. When they couldn't find work in St. John's they moved to Cornwall Bay where there were jobs for two teachers. It was a small place of about 1,000 people, like many Newfoundland outports. It had all the basics and a decent road that led to the main highway that went across the island. As long as you didn't mind driving for six hours, you could get to St. John's with its airport and good shopping. Penny was born in 2003 in the small hospital in Cornwall Bay. That's where she grew up, finished high school, and eventually left to go to St. John's for her post-secondary education. Penny's life growing up was much like any other girl from outport

Newfoundland. It was when she arrived in St. John's that things were different.

****

Staying in the student residence at Memorial had its benefits. You got a bed to sleep in, a closet for your clothes, and a desk to study at and keep your computer, papers, and books in. You could eat at the university dining hall for a set fee and the food was decent and kept you alive. It was secure. But Penny didn't like everything about it. She got one side of the room and a roommate got the other. She was fortunate and got a roommate she liked the first year, but the second year she got Greta Barnes. Greta was in her fourth year and was a stickler for quiet and studying and wouldn't allow any girly horsing around. In her first year Penny was able to bargain with her roommate which nights to let her have the room until after midnight. They both had boyfriends and wanted guaranteed private time in the room on certain nights. And they had all-girl pajama parties with lots of wine. But in that second year everything was different. The room was for sleeping and studying and that's about it according to Greta. Greta didn't have a boyfriend. She used to apparently, but he got fed up with her and went off with someone normal. So,

Penny partied in friends' rooms, and even "rented" a friend's room now and then, as required.

Penny had a boyfriend she met in St. John's that first year. They got along well. Satisfied each other's needs, but neither of them felt it was their final story. He drank too much and did some strong drugs. Penny stayed pretty clean except for some wine and beer. She had fun but she studied and did well. You can't get through engineering without work, no matter how smart you are.

In third year, Penny moved into one of the university-owned apartment buildings. Four people in each apartment, each with their own bedroom, and a common kitchen, dining, living room area. She had broken up with her boyfriend after he got busted dealing drugs. By October she had met Michael Crane and they were getting into each other pretty good. He was from a wealthy family in Carbonear and even took her home to visit them during half-term break in early November. He told her he loved her in December and proposed before they went home for Christmas after the first semester. It was way too fast for Penny. She told him she really liked him but would have to think about it and would let him know when she got back in the New Year.

He snapped the little ring case shut, and left the room,

slamming the door. Penny ran after him, saying she would seriously think about it and didn't want to decide too quickly. She had only known him for a few months, she shouted, but he was gone.

The next day Michael came by early before she left to drive to Cornwall Bay for Christmas. They made up. He apologized for how he responded. He told her he loved her. He hoped for the same confession of love back from her, but it never came.

Penny talked to her mom about the proposal over Christmas. She talked to her friends. But in the end, it was her decision to make. She decided that it was too soon, and she was not sure she loved him. Even though he was from a very well-to-do family, it was not worth it, she decided. She wanted to marry for love, not money.

When she got back to St. John's and gave Michael her answer, she tried to do it as gently as possible. The slap he gave her on her cheek and the punch to her nose were not gentle. They were in his house alone. He lived in a small bungalow his parents had bought for him and his brother while they were at university. She had not thought she needed to be worried about safety when she agreed to go there that evening. She had been many times before. They had had sex there many times.

On this night, though, he dragged her from the living room to his bedroom. He grabbed her hair and shoved her down onto the bed. He hit her in the face again and was about to rip her clothes off when they both heard the door open. It was Michael's brother and his boyfriend. Penny shouted, "Help." And the sound got out before Michael clamped his hand over her face.

Both men rushed into the bedroom. When Michael's brother saw Penny's bloody nose and swollen eye, he grabbed Michael, and said to Penny: "Go. Get your stuff and go, please."

Penny left in a hurry. When she got back to her room it was empty. Her new housemate hadn't arrived yet. She would be arriving the next day. Penny got cleaned up. Her face was badly swollen, and her nose was maybe a bit crooked, but she couldn't tell for sure. The next morning it looked worse and still painful. She thought she should go to the emergency room but she was scared and didn't know what to do. Should she or could she press charges? She mostly wanted to just make the whole situation go away, to put it behind her, to heal. She didn't want to call her parents. They would jump in their car and come to St. John's and go to the police. They would take over. No, she just wanted to cover up in bed and close out the world.

Then the doorbell rang. She was afraid to answer it. Was it Michael wanting to talk, she wondered? Would he be stalking her now? She wanted nothing to do with him. She had decided she would not press charges, but she never wanted to see him again.

The buzzer rang again. More persistent this time. Then a knock on the door and a female voice saying "Hello, anybody in there? I don't have a key."

Penny got off her bed and went to the door. She looked through the peep hole and saw a young woman. She looked a little older than Penny. Penny open the door a crack. "Who are you?"

"It's Leigh Ann Randell. I'm your new housemate."

Penny remembered that one of the girls from last fall would not be returning for the winter term. This must be the new person. "Oh, I'm so sorry it took me so long to answer. Come in." Penny let the door open.

Leigh Ann came through the door; she was dragging two suitcases behind her and had a pack on her back. She looked up at Penny and was about to say "Hello" when something else came out. "My God, what happened?"

Penny ran to her bed and jumped under the covers and turned into the wall sobbing. Leigh Ann finished dragging her cases into the room, closed the door, and said, "What can I do? Can I help? I'm a second-year medical student. Have you had your face looked at or x-rayed?"

Penny thought to herself as she sobbed, I didn't go to medicine, so medicine came to me.

"No," she said through her sobs, "not yet. Should I?"

"Let me see," said Leigh Ann, as she got Penny to sit up on the bed and face her. She touched the swollen cheek. Penny pulled away. She touched her nose and Penny yelped. One eye was swollen shut.

"We're going now," said Leigh Ann. "You need x-rays."

Leigh Ann helped Penny get dressed and bundle up with a coat and hood to obscure her face. They went downstairs and hurried out the door to Penny's car. Leigh Ann didn't have a car, but she had a driver's licence. A few minutes later they were at the emergency room at the Health Sciences Centre. The triage nurse looked at Penny's swollen face and chatted with Leigh Ann, whom she recognized from a rotation in the emergency room a few months before. Penny was called in after about 30 minutes.

The next two hours were a blur. X-rays showed a broken nose, but no displacement so she didn't need surgery. That was good, thought Penny. Facial bones weren't fractured. More good news. Should all heal in time and she would be as beautiful as ever in a few weeks, a well-meaning male medical student told her. She wanted to hit him, but then realized how funny, if inappropriate, that thought was. Then the social worker came in.

Leigh Ann was in the room and the social worker said, "Perhaps you could let me talk to her alone."

"I'd rather she stay," Penny said. "She's the best friend I have right now."

"OK then, that's fine. How are you, sweetie?" she asked.

Penny wanted to hit her also, but knew she was just trying to be nice. "I'm as good as I can be, I guess."

"Did someone do this to you?"

It sounded like a stupid question. She wanted to say, "No, I beat myself up," but instead she got right to the point. "Yes, my boyfriend did it because I refused to marry him. And no, he didn't rape me, but he would have if his brother hadn't come home and pulled him off me."

"When was this?"

"Last night."

"Have you gone to the police?"

"No, and I don't want to. I just want to have this over and done with."

"OK. Are you worried he may try to contact you or come after you again?"

"I don't know. Perhaps," said Penny.

"I'll look out for her," said Leigh Ann. "We're housemates. There are four of us in the apartment, we'll make sure she's safe."

"Does he know where you live?" asked the social worker.

"Yes, but I think I'll be OK. I'll just go home with Leigh Ann now."

The social worker gave her a card with her contact information. When they were in the car, Penny said, "Leigh Ann, I can't thank you enough for your help today. You're going to make a great housemate. If this had been last year, my roommate would have been useless to me."

"Who was your roommate last year? Sounds like you had a problem."

"It was Greta Barnes. She was from Port St. William. We didn't get along well. She was a real prude. Never did anything but study. We shared a room in the residence all second year. She wouldn't let me have guys in to visit. I finally got rid of her by moving into the student apartments." Penny reached over and touched Leigh Ann's arm, and said, "And again, thank you so much for your help."

"Greta Barnes, eh? From Port St. William, eh? Well, I'm Leigh Ann Randell, from Port St. William."

"Oh shit. Do you know Greta? Are you related or something? Fuck I shouldn't have opened my mouth."

"No worries, Penny. You described Greta the way I would. No, we are not related. We were interested in the same guy for a while in high school. He dumped both of us in the end. Anyway, I'm not a prude. I do study a lot … medical school and all. But I start my family medicine rotation tomorrow. I won't be around much except to sleep."

"If there's anything I can do to make your life easier, let me know."

"Listen to you, offering to help me when you're the one in a state. Thanks. But tell me, you were being truthful when you said he didn't rape you, were you Penny?"

"Totally. He was trying to rip my blouse off when his brother came in, but never got further than that. I think the top button on my blouse snapped, but that's it. No, I'm fine, but knowing his intent and what he would have done is scary."

"Do you think he is a rapist and will do that to someone else?"

"Well that's what I keep thinking about. Perhaps I should report him. But I don't want to. I want just to put it behind me and get on with my life."

"I can understand and respect that. You and I have to get to know each other now. Let's go back to our room and I'll order a pizza ."

"That would be great. I think it might hurt some to eat, but I am starving."

"And I have a friend who is an amazing makeup artist. You have to start classes in a few days, and we have to get you looking good."

****

Michael did come looking for her. He harassed her. He said he was sorry and would never do it again. Penny reported him and got a restraining order against him. It took months, but she finally got rid of him and two years later, in the fall of 2027, she went to work for AP Construction after finishing her engineering degree—and met Johnnie. She had not had a boyfriend between Michael and Johnnie. She and Leigh Ann remained good friends. Leigh Ann was delighted when Penny and Johnnie connected. She told Penny about the Saturday morning meetings Johnnie used to have with Uncle John on the wharf to watch the sun come up. She told her how it turned out Johnnie was Uncle John's grandson and he hadn't known it. She told her about the tragedy of little Jason's death and how it might be because Johnnie and his first wife Charlotte were related. So, Penny knew all of this long before Johnny asked her to come to Port St. William with him to meet his family.

Chapter 15
On The Wharf
Saturday, September 16, 2028

"Eh grandfather, I've got a picture but it's mostly the sun coming up through fog," said Johnnie.

"Let me have a look," said Uncle John. He got up close to the camera, and said, "Yip, I've seen many of those over the years. But thanks, Johnnie. I only ever see the sunrise now when you come home and take a picture."

"I hear you're going into the home next week."

"Yes, I am. But not the nursing home, not yet. I'll be where they put people who can still get up and around and get themselves down to the dining room for their meals and who can look after themselves in the bathroom and things like that. Everybody worries about me, Dean and Deanna, and even your father.

"My mind is good, you know. But they worry I might start to forget I turned the stove on, and they worry I might fall and break something, while I'm here alone at night. I told them there was no need to worry but they took me over to see the place and it looks good. I said I'd go if I had my own room. I wasn't going to go buddying up with some old feller, not at my age. There was a private room available and I have some insurance, and some savings and all of that. Anyway, I move on Monday. Next time you bring me a picture you'll have to bring it to the Port St. William Home for Seniors."

There was a knock on the door.

"That's probably Penny. I want you to meet her." Johnnie went and let her in.

"Grandfather, this is the love of my life, Penelope Warren. Penny, meet John Parsons, my grandfather."

"Well hello, young lady, glad to meet you," said Uncle John.

Penny walked over to the chair Uncle John was in and shook his outstretched hand. She could tell it would have been a slow process for him to stand up.

"Good to meet you sir. Johnnie is always talking about you."

"Mostly lies, I'm sure. Most of what I have told him over the years is only half true. He just can't figure out which half. But my, you do remind me of someone. You ever been around here or have any family from around here?"

"No, don't think so, sir. I grew up on the west coast, Cornwall Bay."

"Nope, never been there and don't know anyone from

there," said Uncle John.

"So, what shall I call you, sir? Uncle John, I guess."

"That sounds just fine to me," said Uncle John. "Unless you marry this young feller and then you can call me grandfather like he does."

"Well, we'll have to wait I guess, he hasn't proposed yet. I don't know what's stopping him."

"Jazus, Johnnie. Did you hear that? Man, get on with it and grab this woman as fast as you can while she's in the receptive mood."

"She's just getting on with you, grandfather. We've already talked about getting married. I'm just waiting to save a bit more money so I can get the ring she deserves."

"Yes, well all very sensible of you two. But gosh you do remind me of someone. Just can't place it. Warren ... What was your mother's maiden name?"

"She was a Ryan from St. John's. But there are Ryans all over the island. My father grew up in St. John's. He was a Warren, of course."

"So, you're a dyed-in-the-wool townie then?"

"Well my parents are from town, but I grew up in Cornwall Bay, as I said. They moved there after they finished university to teach, and stayed. They're still in Cornwall Bay now. I think my grandparents or great-grandparents came in from out around the bay many years ago. So, I guess my family has been back and forth between the bay and town. Who knows what I am?" She laughed. "It seems the whole island is moving to St. John's, these days though."

"Yes, that's true," said Uncle John.

"OK then," said Johnnie. "We need to be going. I think Leigh Ann wants to introduce you to all her friends. You girls are having a get together or something tonight at her parents' place, is that right?"

"Yes, that's right'" said Penny.

"OK then, see ya grandfather. I won't see you until the next time I'm back home." He went over and gave him a hug.

Penny went over to shake his hand. Uncle John stood up, reached out to hug her, and said, "Check to see if there was a Samantha Penelope Ryan in your family way back. You know, around 80 years ago."

Johnnie thought for a second, and said, "Didn't you tell me a story about her back when I was teenager. And didn't you say …"

Uncle John interpreted him, "Now Johnnie, you know half the stuff I told you wasn't true."

Johnnie looked at him and smiled. "OK, grandfather, I'll leave it there."

Chapter 16
Digging Into The Past
Spring 2029

"How are you finding work at AP?" asked Johnnie as they sat back from the dinner table. Johnnie and Penny were engaged and living together. Johnnie had finally saved enough to get the ring he wanted. Or really the one Penny wanted. The wedding date was set for 2030. They had agreed they weren't going to plan anything big.

"It's not bad," said Penny. "I don't like what I'm doing as much as you seem to like what you're doing, but I'm OK."

"That's good. Who knows, something else might come up with AP or another company."

"I'm fine for now. What I am really getting into right now though is my genealogy, as you know. On my father's side the Warrens have been traced back for centuries, so I have lots of information there. But my mother's family is a little hazy."

"How so?" asked Johnnie.

"My mother's parents both died while I was in junior high school. They were in their 60s. I recall them but not clearly anymore. They died in a motor vehicle accident in Florida while on vacation. They were Jonathan and Susie Ryan. I think she had some Chinese in her background, but I am not sure how much or where from. Probably not from Newfoundland, but who knows. I cannot find anything in my grandmother's past. Same for my grandfather. He seems to have appeared out of nowhere. I can't find any records. I can't find birth certificates for either of them."

"That's strange. Maybe they weren't born in Newfoundland. You should talk to your mother," suggested Johnnie.

"I did that. I called her last week. She said we would talk about it when I came to visit next. My mother never really talked about her family's past. It always seemed to be taboo. All we knew growing up is that our families were from St. John's and we now lived in Cornwall Bay. We didn't get into St. John's to see them much. By the time I got to St. John's to go to university my grandparents were dead."

"We're going to Cornwall Bay for Easter, right?" said Johnnie.

"Yes, and I'll try to get her to open up as much as possible. You're meeting my mom and dad for the first time on that trip too, remember?"

****

"You stay here," said Penny as she went into her parent's house, leaving Johnnie out on the doorstep.

"Jeremy, see who's at the door. It might be Penny," came a voice from the kitchen.

Her father came to the foyer from the living room. "Hello, my lovely girl, come on in." He gave her a hug and a kiss. Her mother was there by now, wiping her hands in her apron.

"Hello darling, how are you." Another hug and kiss. "So, where's this Johnnie of yours?"

"Now before you get on me about being engaged and living with someone before you guys even met him, I want to say I'm sorry, but it's a long way to Cornwall Bay from St. John's and things moved quickly and we are in love."

"Oh, stop it. It's fine. But where is he?"

"He's outside. I wanted to get this over with first."

"What?" said her father. "You left him out on the step? Let the poor man in."

Jeremy Warren opened the door. Johnnie was standing there quietly and when the door opened, he said, "Mr. Warren, I presume."

"Well, Mr. Parsons. I hear you plan to take our

daughter away."

"Only if she will come willingly, sir." Johnnie held out his hand and his future father-in-law shook it.

"Come in Johnnie. Penny shouldn't have left you outside like this."

"No problem. At least it's not raining, and you have a lovely view of the bay from your front step." Johnnie stepped into the house.

After dinner, Jeremy took Johnnie out to look around the three-acre lot, while Penny and her mother chatted.

"Mom, I've been trying to research our family tree and I seem to get stuck getting back past grandma and grandpa on your side. I can't find much about them or where they came from. Who their parents were. Things like that."

"Oh, dear, Penny. I knew this day would come, but to tell you the truth, I don't know a lot either."

"Well start with grandpa," said Penny. "His name was Jonathon Ryan. There is no birth certificate that I could find."

"There is none that anyone can find, sweetie. I looked after their deaths but couldn't find anything. I think it was lost or never recorded in the first place. It was as if there was something to hide. I do remember mom telling me that dad's family came from a small place around the bay. But that his mother, when she was pregnant, came to St. John's to have him and never went back home. She said his mother, who would be your great-grandmother, never told her anything about her family or about who the father of her child was."

"Wow, that's confusing," said Penny, getting her pen and paper out. "So, let's see. There's me, and there's you, my mother, then there's your father, my grandfather, Jonathan Ryan. We think his mother, whose name we are not sure of, came from around the bay, presumably pregnant, to have her baby in St. John's. Presumably she had her baby, your father that is, in St. John's but we can't find any record."

"That is all true dear, except we do know my grandmother's name. It was Samantha, she went by Sam so that causes things to get confused at times. But, yes, she was Samantha Penelope Ryan. I named you after her. I liked the name Penelope a lot."

"My God," said Penny. "Johnnie's grandfather told me to look for a Samantha Penelope Ryan when I was looking back into my family history, but he didn't say why. I wonder where she was from. Uncle John must know her. We'll have to ask him. But that also means she might be from Port St. William or around there somewhere."

"Oh, I remember father mentioning that place, Port

St. William, but I can't recall now in what context."

"OK mom, thanks. Now what about your mother, Susie? She was Susie Ryan because she married Jonathan Ryan, but what was her maiden name?"

"She was Susie Wong, before she married my father."

"Sounds Chinese."

"Yes, it is Chinese. And I think that's why it wasn't talked about much in our family. I am ashamed now, for feeling like I had to hide my Asian heritage. Her father must have been Caucasian, I think. She didn't seem to know anything about him. You will notice that I have some Asian facial features, as well. You do too, but they're subtle. Most people don't notice."

"Do you know where your mother came from. How did she get here?"

"She came from Toronto, I think, to go to school at Memorial University in the 1970s. While she never said anything about her father, she did tell me that her mother's name was Chen. I named you after both your great-grandmothers. Our past was so blurred it was the only way I knew to help preserve it. I put it in your name. So, you are Penelope Chen Warren. Soon to be Penelope Chen Hawkins, I assume."

****

A couple of days later Penny and Johnnie drove back to St. John's from Cornwall Bay. Penny was determined to dig deeper into her past. She had to find out more about Samantha Penelope Ryan, who she was, where she was from, and who was the father of her child. The child that was her grandfather, Jonathan Ryan. She also had to see if she could find out who Chen Wong was, where she was from, and who had fathered her child. The child that was her grandmother, Susie Wong.

Chapter 17
Samantha Penelope Ryan

In the coolness of the evening, after a hot summer day in 1955, Samantha sat on a stool in her father's shed. A rope hung around a beam and one end was tied into a hangman's noose. It wasn't a well-tied noose, but it looked like it would serve the purpose. Below the noose was a chair. Trembling, Samantha struggled to get up on the chair. She almost tipped the chair over on her first try, but eventually made it. Samantha stood on the chair for a while and then stuck her head in the noose and pulled it tight.

It had been a long journey to this point. As a child, Sam had been like most other girls. It wasn't until she reached her early and mid-teenage years that she realized she felt different than her friends about many things. She was attracted to boys, but she wasn't going crazy about them like most of the other girls her age. And she was also attracted to girls. Not just in a friendly, get-together-and-talk-about-boys sort of way, but in the same way that the other girls talked about boys. She felt something that she didn't fully understand when she saw or talked about girls. She didn't know what was happening and she was afraid. She felt different.

Sam went out with a few boys during her teenage years but nothing serious, nothing sexual. She never did find a girl who had the same inclinations as she did. That just confirmed how different she was. Later Sam realized there probably had been other girls who felt the same, but like Sam, they were afraid. In the 1940s, homosexuality was not only not understood or accepted, it was illegal. And being different was not acceptable. Germans were different, Japanese were different, to be different was to be bad. So, Sam tried to keep herself as un-different as possible. All the time yearning for the girls she saw around her, but never able to be who she was.

She liked one boy, John Parsons. She thought she might be able to have a relationship with him. But it never happened. They were friends only, and when John went away to Toronto, they kept in touch by mail. In fact, they wrote a lot of letters back and forth. John got himself in trouble and it was several years before he got out of prison and returned home.

Now, standing on the chair in her father's shed, with a noose around her neck, ready to end it all, Sam thought of the past few months. John had returned home from Ontario and they rekindled their old friendship. A friendship that had been kept alive for three years by letters back and forth. During the past months since John returned, they had spent days talking about what it was like in prison, about Sam's job as a teacher, and about their families and their plans. Skirting the idea that they might have a future together as something more then friends. They grew close and then just 24 hours before Sam walked into her fathers shed, they had made love.

Sam enjoyed the lovemaking, but she knew it would not be enough for her. She knew she would need intimacy with women as well. If she married John, she knew she would likely eventually find a woman and cheat on him. Sam became so distraught with what she saw in her future and that she would eventually hurt John, she decided to take her own life. To end it all.

She wrote a letter, put it in an envelope addressed to John, and set it on the worktable in the shed. The letter told him that she loved him. It explained how she felt about women. It said she feared she would never be able to be completely faithful to him because she would want intimacy with women. She apologized for what she was about to do but felt it was the only way out for her and was the best for him.

But the rope broke, or the knot slipped, or something. Sam ended up in a heap on the floor. Her neck was sore because the rope burned as it came unraveled. She lay on the floor with her knees pulled up to her chin for hours. She sobbed. She was angry she couldn't even kill herself properly. Then she decided: if she couldn't run away from all of life, she would at least run away from the life she had. The life that didn't let her be who she really was. She would run away and cut ties with everyone from Harbour Devon, everyone she knew. She would kill herself after all. She would be dead to this life.

Sam took the letter sitting on the table and, without opening it, wrote on the outside of the envelope. "I couldn't do what I set out to do. I love you John, but I will never see you again. Goodbye." She read what she had written on the outside and then set the envelope back down on the table and went out into the darkness.

When Samantha Penelope Ryan left the shed that night, she didn't leave alone. Samantha didn't know she was pregnant.

Sam packed a small bag and the next morning, before anyone was up, she took her father's boat with an outboard motor to Port St. William and caught the coastal boat from there. By late that evening she was in St. John's, the last half of the journey being by taxi.

****

Three years later, Sam called from the washroom, "Rhonda, could you get Jonathan? I think he's finished his nap."

"Why you got pregnant and kept that kid, Sam, I'll never know." Rhonda mumbled under her breath, as she got up off the sofa and walked into the little bedroom in their apartment where Jonathan slept in a crib.

The toddler, in the midst of the terrible twos, stopped crying when he saw Rhonda open the door. He smiled and jumped up and down in his crib, holding onto the rails. "Womda, Womda," he said, and held out his hands.

"You are a cute little rascal," she said, grabbing him under his arms and pulling him into her chest. A few seconds later he squirmed to get down and then ran off with a soggy diaper, looking for his toys.

"You need to be changed," said Rhonda, walking after him. "But I'll let your mother do that."

Rhonda had been a nurse in the hospital when Sam delivered her baby two years before. They got along well, and kept in touch after Sam was discharged. Sam was on welfare, barely able to pay for a single room in a boarding house for her and her new baby. Within a month, Sam and Jonathan had moved in with Rhonda, and a month later, Sam and Rhonda were lovers. Rhonda's house had two bedrooms. At first Sam and Jonathan shared a bedroom. After a while, Sam moved in with Rhonda and Jonathan slept in the other room.

They were officially life partners. But to the outside world and to friends, they were close friends, sharing accommodations.

Samantha was thankful for Rhonda's help. She liked Rhonda a lot. She enjoyed the sex, she had a place for herself and little Jonathan, but she felt guilty because she didn't love Rhonda, at least not the way Rhonda loved her. Rhonda put up with Jonathan because she loved Sam. She helped with Jonathan's care, because she loved Sam. She didn't charge Sam any rent because she loved her, and Sam didn't have any money anyway. The bit of money Sam did get from welfare went to looking after little Jonathan's needs. Rhonda had a good job as a nurse. It was all working out, for now.

This went on until Jonathan was six and had to go to school. To Jonathan everything was quite normal. Samantha was "Mommy," Rhonda was "Aunt Rhonda," he slept in his room and Mommy and Aunt Rhonda slept together in the other room. But within three months of Jonathan going to school, his very conservative teacher reported what Jonathan was saying to a social worker. Marion Cunningham visited Jonathan and his mommy and aunt Rhonda at their house.

"My goodness," said Rhonda, "what are you suggesting? There's nothing unusual going on at all. Samantha and I are just good friends. She was in a difficult position when she had Jonathan and so I let her move in with me. She pays rent every month from her welfare cheque and helps with the food. She doesn't have much, but she does what she can.

"We sleep in the same bed, but there is nothing going on like you are suggesting. The other bedroom is small so little Jonathan sleeps there and we share the larger bed in the larger room. But my goodness there is nothing of the sort going on that you are implying."

"OK then," said Marion, shaking her long curly red hair, and looking more bored than interested in this particular home visit. "I'll look around, if I may, and if everything seems to be as you say, I'll make my report and say things are fine."

And that was what happened. The report stated that nothing was illegal about Samantha and Rhonda's relationship. The school was satisfied, and all the other children and their mothers were satisfied, and life carried on.

Chapter 18
Jonathan and Susie

Jonathan was always first in his class in school. He graduated from high school in 1973 and, two years later, was accepted into medicine at the new Memorial University Faculty of Medicine.

"You little brat, you're gonna make something of yourself after all," said Rhonda, giving him a hug and rubbing his head.

"I told you Rhonda. I told you our baby boy was going to make it big someday," said his mother.

"Now guys, I have a lot ahead of me. I got into medical school. Now I have to get out the other end with a licence. That takes at least five years, and that's if I want to be a GP. A specialist would take another four years past that."

"I suppose you think you'll be an old man by the time you finish. Sure, even if you become a specialist, you'll only be 28 or 29. Still in your 20s for god's sake. Your mother and I are 45 and we're not old. Well, I'm not old. Are you old, Sam?" she asked her partner with a laugh.

"How can I feel old today? Look what I produced. Me

and my John. A young man with a wonderful life ahead of him. No not old today. I feel as young as the day I made you my son."

"And I feel as old as the day I delivered you. Because I did, you know. The doctor didn't make it until after you were all cuddled in a blanket on your mother's belly. Your mother and that John guy might have made you, but I pulled you out into the world." Rhonda gave him another hug.

"Mom, someday you got to tell me about John. You never have," said Jonathan.

"No need to son. He provided the sperm, that's all."

"Why won't you talk about him? Was he hard on you or something?"

"Oh my. No. Please never think it was like that. John was the kindest man I have ever known. I loved him. You are a love child, but ... well you know."

"Maybe I should try to find him someday," said Jonathan.

"Don't ever do that, son. Just be satisfied knowing he is a good man. He has a family of his own now, I suspect. He never even knew I was pregnant. He doesn't know anything about you. Please leave it at that."

"Why, was he married to someone else when you got

pregnant. Was it an affair?"

Sam looked at her son. "I will tell you he was not married or even in a relationship with anyone else when we were together. But that's all I'm saying, Jon. Please leave it. And, so you know, John is not even his real name. That's all I'm saying."

"I don't even know who your father is, sweetie," said Rhonda. "And I don't know his real name either. So, don't be asking me any questions. I think she is protecting the man. From what, I don't know."

"OK," said Sam, "Nuf of this. Let's open a bottle of wine."

****

In 1977, Jonathan met Susie Wong, a woman of Caucasian-Chinese ancestry from Toronto who was three years older than him. She had come to Memorial University several years before to study Geography and Marine Biology. In 1978 they married.

During the one-year courtship and engagement, Jonathan Ryan tried to find out as much as he could about the woman he was going to marry.

"What do you mean you don't know your mother?"

asked Jon.

"I mean I wouldn't recognize her if I saw her on the street. I mean, if she came to visit claiming she was my mother, I would have to ask her to prove it with some documents or pictures or something. I think the last time I saw her was when I was about five years old. I only know that because my grandparents, who raised me, told me she had left when I was about two years old and then showed up again when I was five years old for a week or two, and then they never saw her again. They have never told me anything about her except her name. Her name was Chen, Chen Wong. I was given her surname, not my father's. I have no idea who my father was, not even his name. I don't know his name. All I know is that he must have been white because, well, look at me."

Jon smiled, "And so lovely to look at you are. God, I love you. I don't care who your parents were."

"You're sweet. But I know you. You're just trying to get my panties off again. Maybe I should go celibate until you make me an honest woman."

"Oh, please don't. I'll die. It's another whole three months before the wedding."

"Back in the day Jonnie boy, men had to wait until

the night of the wedding, like it or lump it."

"Well I don't like the way it was back in the day."

She poked him and smiled, and said, "I don't like the old ways either."

"I have a condom," he said.

"Don't need it," she said. "I started on the pill six weeks ago. Just didn't tell you. I was going to keep it as a wedding gift – "no condom sex," I mean—but I can't wait either."

He grabbed her and carried her to their bedroom.

Later, lying in bed, he said, "Your grandparents raised you, right."

"Yes, that's right."

"So, what were their names?"

"I called my grandmother "Ama" and my grandfather "gong-gong.""

"That's like nanny and poppy. Short for grandmother and grandfather. Is that right?"

"Yes. Her actual name was Ah Lam Wong and my grandfather was Chao Wong."

"You have been in St. John's for five years now, right?"

"Yes."

"When did you last see them?"

"Two years ago. I went back to Toronto for their funeral. They died in a fire."

"Oh my God, Susie. I didn't know. You never mentioned it before."

"It's hard to think about them. They raised me. I am Chao and Ah Lam's daughter as far as I'm concerned. My biological mother means nothing to me really. It is as if she never existed."

They rolled over and went to sleep.

***

A week or two later, it was Susie's turn to inquire about family histories. "We talked a lot about my family a couple of weeks ago," she said to Jonathan, "but what about yours? I know Samantha and Rhonda."

"Yes, mom and some guy whose name may be John made me, as mom says, and Rhonda pulled me into the world, as she claims. They're my parents. I love them both even with all their quirks, and their bitching, and their jabs at each other."

"Do you know anything about your mom's parents or about this John guy?"

"Not a lot. I remember a conversation with mom a few years ago. I tried to get her to tell me about her past. She said both her parents were dead and that she had not been back to the small community she grew up in since she left. She won't tell me which community that is, and she won't tell me the name of the man who made her pregnant. She says he was a nice man, but she has had no contact with him since the night they had sex. She begged me not to try to find him. She said he probably did not even know she was pregnant when she left and came to St. John's."

"Wow, so that's it. That's all you know?"

"Yep. That's it."

"I think when we get married, we will have to start this new family of ours from scratch," said Susie. "There's not much of a past on either of our sides, is there?

"From this point on we need to bring as much normalcy to our lives as we can. If people will let us."

Susie looked at him. "What do you mean, Jon, if people will let us?"

"Well, interracial marriages are not exactly common in Newfoundland. We may face bigotry."

"That's true, but times are changing, and I think Newfoundland is different that way than many places."

"Perhaps. We have two dysfunctional families behind us, but in front of us there is the potential for a bright future. We'll be well educated. Hopefully we'll make good money and have lots of beautiful children."

"Good idea my love. Let's go make one of those beautiful children now." She smiled, stood up, and took him by the hand. "However, I'm still on the pill, so making a baby will be difficult – but we can try really hard anyway."

****

In 1980, when Jon was in the middle of his internship, Susie delivered their first child. They named her Wendy. Little Wendy Ryan was 7 pounds 2 ounces and very healthy.

In 2002, Wendy married Jeremy Warren and a year later they had a baby girl. Wendy searched deep into her ancestry for names for the child. She didn't know much about either of her grandmothers. Her father's mother died when Wendy was just 10 years old and she couldn't really remember much about her. She knew her name was Samantha Penelope Ryan. She knew almost nothing about her mother's mother except her name. In the end she decided on Penelope Chen—Chen to recognize her Chinese ancestry even though her little girl, Penelope Chen Warren, had very few if any distinguishable Asian features.

Chapter 19
On The Wharf
August 2029

The summer of 2029 was a hot one. Uncle John was 99 years old and in the Port St. William Home for Seniors. Penny and Johnnie were home. They had decided to get married in Port St. William. The first Saturday after arriving there, Johnnie and Penny went down to the wharf and recorded a video of one of the most beautiful sunrises Johnnie had ever seen.

"Look at this, grandfather," said Johnnie, holding up his tablet. "It's one of the best."

Uncle John was entranced by the five-minute video. "It reminds me of a sunrise from many years ago." A tear ran down his face. "Oh, don't mind me crying," he said. "I'm just a sentimental old man these days."

"It's so beautiful, it's enough to make you cry," said Penny.

"You're a sweetie my dear. You have a good one here, Johnnie."

"Thanks, Uncle John, but I think I have a pretty good catch, too," said Penny.

"And that you do, my dear. Anyway, Penny I have to ask you." Uncle John wiped his nose. "Did you find a Samantha Penelope Ryan in your search into the past?"

"I did, Uncle John. And I think she was from here in Port St. William."

"No, not from here, from Harbour Devon up the shore a bit."

"Did you know her?" asked Penny.

"Yes," said Uncle John, and he started to tear again.

"Grandfather. You told me about Sam. You told me she hung herself."

"I guess I lied to you, Johnnie. Although it wasn't really a lie, just a limited version of what happened."

Uncle John went over to his dresser and pulled an envelope out from underneath some clothes. He came back and sat in his chair and told them the story of that night and Sam's decision to leave Harbour Devon forever. Then he took the letter out of the envelope and gave them the letter to read.

"So, she did kill herself," said Johnnie.

Then he gave them the envelope. They read what was on the outside.

'She didn't kill herself," said Penny. "She ran away.

Probably to St. John's. You think?"

"Yes, that's exactly what happened," said Uncle John. "And she was pregnant with our child."

Johnnie's face went pale. "Not again, grandfather. Not again. Not the same thing all over again."

"I'm pretty sure Penny is my great-granddaughter. I had heard rumors, about 10 years after she left, that she had a child, but I didn't know the timing of it. It was possible, I thought, that she was not pregnant when she left and got pregnant later. But to be honest, I doubt she was ever with a man again after me. I'm not being cocky saying that. It's just that I know how she felt.

"Then in 1992 I received a letter from a Rhonda Hogan telling me Sam had died of a stroke just two years before, when she was 60. She told me that Sam had confided in her just a year before she died and told her the whole story of our relationship and her coming to St. John's. Apparently, Rhonda was her life partner. They had raised Sam's child as their own. His name was Jonathon. So, he would have been Jonathan Ryan, not Jonathan Parsons. I replied to the letter, but it was returned. I discovered later that Rhonda died a year after she sent the letter, in 1993. She had committed suicide. I guess she had succeeded where Sam had failed."

"My mother was a Ryan before she married my father," said Penny. "Her father's name was Jonathan Ryan and she thinks his mother was Samantha Penelope Ryan. That could all be true, and Jonathan's father might not be you. But the timing is right. He was born in 1956. And that letter from Rhonda pretty much confirms it."

Uncle John cried. "Yes, Sam's son was mine. I know it because I saw her in your eyes the first time I met you. You belong to her. And I think you belong to me. Sam and I are your great-grandparents"

"Grandfather, you know what Charlotte and I went through and how that turned out. I can't do it again."

Johnnie got up and left. He was crying.

Uncle John looked at Penny. "Let him go. He needs time. He's afraid, Penny. He thinks little Jason's heart problem and his death was all due to him and Charlotte being related. If I am your great-grandfather, then you and Johnnie are related in exactly the same way as Johnnie and Charlotte were related. And I think with great certainty I am."

"I know. Johnnie and I have spent many hours talking about his marriage to Charlotte and the worries they had. He told me about the visit to the geneticist and the reassurance that everything would be OK. He talked about watching their little one getting sicker and sicker and dying. He's not over it. May never be. And now this happening. Johnnie and I talked about how we were not related and how it was likely there wasn't even a very distant relationship.

"And now it looks like we are related just like he and Charlotte were. Your life is coming back to affect everyone in your family, Uncle John. Or I suppose I can call you grandfather now, even before Johnnie and I get married."

"I have wondered this myself," said Uncle John. "I have thought about it and read about it many times. The Bible says in the old testament as part of the very first commandment, *for I the* LORD *your God am a jealous God, visiting the iniquity of the fathers on the children to the third and the fourth generation.* But in other places in the Bible it says that this is not so, that we will pay for our own sins only. In Ezekiel it says, *The soul who sins shall die. The son shall not suffer for the iniquity of the father, nor the father suffer for the iniquity of the son. The righteousness of the righteous shall be upon himself, and the wickedness of the wicked shall be upon himself.* So, the Bible goes both ways, as it often does. I don't know if all of this is because of my sins in the past or not. It never felt like sin at the time. It felt like love."

"I have to go find Johnnie now, grandfather," said

Penny. "We'll be back."

****

"Penny, it's all coming back to me," said Johnnie. He was sitting on a bench on the wharf where he sat every Saturday morning when he was home. The sun was high in the sky. Johnnie was crying. "I just can't go through that again, Penny. I can't."

"What are you saying, Johnnie?"

"I think I'm saying we can't have children. I love you Penny, but I'm afraid. Not of marrying you but of having children with you."

"But I want children, Johnnie. I want you and I want us to have a family."

"Perhaps we could adopt," said Johnnie.

"Perhaps, but it's not the same."

"I know. I'm just afraid of what will happen to the child. It was awful before, Penny. I wouldn't want you to go through it either."

"Can we take it one step at a time? I don't think there's any point getting tested. Uncle John is sure, and he says he can see her in my eyes and has from the first time he saw me. I know he's right. So, let's just accept that it's true.

He's my great-grandfather and your grandfather. We know you and Charlotte were told the risk was not more than in the general population. It might be that you and Charlotte just got unlucky."

"I don't know, Penny. The geneticist might have been wrong."

"Yes, I suppose," said Penny. "But can we just get married and start from there? I want to have a family, Johnnie, but most of all I want to be with you. Will you still marry me?"

"Of course, I will. Let's try to forget about this and get married. But will you always feel this way when the time comes? When we start thinking about children again?"

"I can't think about that now, Johnnie. Let's just finish planning our wedding, get married, and get on with life. It's only two weeks, you know, from the appointed time."

****

Two days later, Johnnie was walking along Water Street in Port St. William on his way to the store to pick up wedding decorations for the church hall. Penny's mother and father were in town from Cornwall Bay. They were with

Johnnie's parents and Penny getting to know each other, planning, and making decisions. Johnnie was the errand boy, doing as he was told. Halfway down Water Street he met Charlotte coming the other way.

"Charlotte, I was so surprised when you accepted the invitation to the wedding ... But I'm glad," said Johnnie. They hugged, a little awkwardly.

"I was just as surprised as you, I guess, Johnnie. At first, I wasn't going to come but ..." She paused. "You and I were only married for two years, Johnnie, but those two years were the hardest either of us will ever experience in our lives. I think, I hope, we will always have that between us, regardless of how hard it was, or how long we live, or who we are with. Little Jason was ours. We'll never forget his short life."

Johnnie's head fell for a second and then he looked up at her, remembering the love they used to have, and feeling great respect for her. She was exactly right. They shared two years that would never be forgotten. Johnnie hugged her again. "Thank you, Charlotte. I feel the same way."

"So how are you, Johnnie? Excited about your wedding?"

"Yes, of course. But I guess it's mainly the bride's show, you know. Us grooms just worry about the speech we have to give. It was the same when we got married, I remember. So yeah, I'm fine. But, how are you? Are you with anyone?"

"I'm in Fort Mac now. Did you know?"

"Yes, I had heard."

"I've been seeing a guy for a year." We're living together."

"I'm glad."

"I should tell you that I have had two miscarriages in the past six months. It's terrible, Johnnie. Not like losing a child. I was early on. About 10 weeks. But we still grieve the loss."

"I'm sure it is. You shouldn't have to go through that sort of grief so many times. I am so sorry."

"Thanks Johnnie, but I bring it up because I'm wondering that maybe Jason's heart problems had nothing to with you and I being related. Perhaps it was just me, and I have a genetic problem and can't have normal babies, so they miscarry. Apparently its nature's way of decreasing the number of abnormal babies being born."

"Oh, Charlotte, don't put all the blame on yourself.

Jason was made from both of us."

"I know, but I just thought I would tell you in case you were worried about the health of the children you and Penny might have. In case you wondered if it was somehow you that led to Jason's problems."

"I appreciate that, Charlotte. But, as I said, he was from both of us. Let's keep it that way. We owned him, we loved him, we will remember him forever as our child."

"Thanks Johnnie. You're a good man. I must go now. I'm off to see my grandparents."

Johnnie hugged her again and watched her walk away. Then he let his heart feel happiness. Maybe he and Penny were not at risk after all. Maybe it was something about Charlotte and not their mixture of genes. Maybe it had nothing to do with Uncle John. He felt guilty for feeling relieved. He felt sad for Charlotte, but happy for him and Penny. He would have to tell Penny as soon as he could.

****

The wedding went as weddings go. Penny was beautiful. Johnnie was nervous. And the new in-laws were proud, and no doubt anticipating grandchildren. Life goes on.

Penny got pregnant. She was due in October 2030.

Chapter 20
Chen Wong's Story

Uncle John, 100 years old now, received a letter in the mail. It was addressed to *Mr. Parsons at the Port St. William Home for Seniors.* There was no other Mr. Parsons besides Uncle John at the home.

Once a week on Sundays, Spencer Hawkins, 61, came to the home to visit his aging father, read to him, and open his mail if there was any.

On a Sunday in July 2030, Spencer read the letter his father had received.

"Dad, this letter is from a Mrs. Chen Hawkins from Toronto. She says she will be visiting you here in the home on August 17. She says she would like your grandson Johnnie Hawkins to be present and his wife, Penny Hawkins. She also wants me there. I don't know of any Chen in our family so I guess it's another Hawkins family."

Uncle John's mind was still very much alert despite his age and his failing physical ability and eyesight. But he did find he had to think about things for a while to make sure they were right in his mind.

"I knew a Chen Wong many years ago. Maybe she

married a Hawkins feller and changed her name. She would be nearly my age now though. Maybe 97 or 98 years old or something like that. I wonder what she wants after all of these years?"

"I guess we let Johnnie and Penny know," said Spencer, "and see what they want to do. Penny is six months pregnant; she may not want to travel next month."

"Let them know," said Uncle John. He thought for a minute. "And tell them I think they should come. I think I may know what this is about, and it may concern them."

****

"Go to Port St. William next month?" said Penny. "What for? It's such a long drive. I'm not sure I want to."

"I know," said Johnnie, "but apparently grandfather wants us to come. It's about a letter he received and a woman who is coming to visit him. The woman asked that we be present. And get this, the woman's name is Chen Hawkins. I wonder if she is the Chen you are named after?"

"Oh, wow, that's interesting then. Tell your father we'll be there."

****

"I have no idea what it's about," said Ted Hawkins to his brother Ben, "but she says she'll be visiting Uncle John Parsons on August 17 at the home and she wants us there."

"Do you recall Dad ever mentioning this woman?" asked Ben.

"No never, but her last name is Hawkins, so I suppose she's related in some way. I went over to see if Uncle John knew anything about it and apparently, he also got a letter. Spencer was invited in that letter instead of ours. So, this Chen person must know Spencer is our half-brother. Who outside our family or a few other people in Port St. William would know that? Anyway, John said he might remember somebody by the name of Chen from when he was in Toronto in the early 1950s."

"Well I guess we go and find out what it's all about," said Ben.

****

On August 17, 2030 a large black Cadillac made the left turn off the highway and drove slowly through the community of Port St. William. It stopped in front of the main entrance to the Port St. William Home for Seniors.

From the front passenger's side, a man in a black suit got out and walked into the home and spoke with the woman at the reception desk. From the driver's side in the back seat another man, dressed in a navy polo shirt and beige pants, got out of the car and walked around the back of the car and opened the back door on the passenger's side. An electric motor could be heard and a wheelchair with an old woman sitting in it slowly moved out from the car and lowered to the ground. The woman manipulated the electronic controls and the wheelchair rolled off the platform and up the ramp to the entrance door. The man in the polo shirt opened the door and she went in. The driver drove the car to a parking spot that had *reserved* written on it, got out of the car, and stood by it.

Inside, the man in black said, "They have all gathered in the meeting room waiting for you. This lady will take us to the room."

The lady behind the desk waved for them to follow her. She led them down a hallway and showed them into the room. "Your visitors have arrived, Uncle John," she said, and left.

****

Inside the room, the family sat around a rectangular

meeting table. Ted and Ben Hawkins, sons of Sarah and Fred Hawkins, were on one side, and Spencer, Johnnie, and Penny Hawkins on the other. Uncle John Parsons was sitting at one end, his wheelchair parked up by the wall behind him. The man in black rolled Chen Hawkins' wheelchair up to the end of the table opposite Uncle John, removed the chair that was there, and rolled the wheelchair into the end of the table. The man in the polo shirt sat in a chair beside the elderly woman. The man in black moved back, closed the door to the room, and stood by it.

Chen placed her hands on the table and said, "My name is Chen Hawkins. In many ways you are all my family. I have a story to tell that will be meaningful to all of you."

****

She told her story up to when Uncle John went to prison. Johnnie had already heard that part from Uncle John years before and most of the others in the room had some familiarity with it. Chen carried on.

"At this point my grandfather was in jail and would later die there. My cousins and brothers were also in jail and my boyfriend Peter Zhang had run away and I never saw him again. It was just me and my parents and the laundry business. And I was visibly pregnant." She looked at Uncle John.

"It had to have been your child, John, because I was not having sex with Peter Zhang, he was too afraid of my grandfather who said he would do terrible things to him if he had sex with me."

"But Chen, what about Fred Hawkins and the policeman? Fred told me all about it when he came to visit me in prison," said Uncle John.

"Those were lies, Johnnie. Lies to make you believe that the child I was carrying was probably not yours. Not that Fred wanted that baby for himself, but rather he just wanted you to stay out of his life. I didn't find out about what he told you at the prison visit until later. The truth is, after the time you and I and Fred met in the restaurant, I did not see Fred again until after the trial and you were in prison. He would not possibly be the father because I was already pregnant. As for my affair with the policeman, it never happened. A kind older policeman helped me a lot during that time, but there was never an affair."

"OK, then," said Uncle John, "so Susie was definitely my daughter."

"Yes, she was," said Chen.

Penny mumbled to Johnnie under her breath, "We have to think about this. Is this possible?"

"Let's just let her finish," said Johnnie.

Chen continued.

"It is what happened in the years after the trial and up to Fred Hawkins' death that affects most people here today. Fred came to see me when I was about four months pregnant. We became very close and were intimate. After the baby was born, I lived with my mother and father for two years raising Susie. Fred continued on the lake boats and would visit me at the beginning and end of each of his three months contracts with the lake boat company. He didn't tell me about his relationship with Sarah White, your mother, at that time." Chen looked over at Ted and Ben.

"Fred convinced me to leave Susie with my parents and to move into our own place. He said we should break off with my Chinese family and start out on our own. That is what I did and apart from one visit with my parents when Susie was five years old, I never saw her alive again. However, I was at her funeral 14 years ago in St. John's. You were there as well Johnnie, or Uncle John as you are called now, but you didn't recognize me. I was sitting behind you in church." Chen paused.

"To continue my story. My parents raised Susie and she moved to Newfoundland and found a life there. In 1955 Fred and I married. By then he was no longer with the lake boats, he had a job in Toronto. He would marry Sarah White seven years later. Fred continued with the story of working on the lake boats until 1989 when he was 58 years old. In that year he retired, and I never saw him again. I know he lived for another nine years and died in 1998 when he was 67 years old." She looked over at Ted and Ben, and then continued.

"Fred lived a double life. I'm sure you must wonder how he could do this. I knew some things about it, but not the full picture until long after he died. When Fred and I married, he used an incorrect name and a false birth date on the certificates. Fred told me there was a woman named Sarah White back in Port St. William who he had a relationship with. He was told she had a baby by him and the reason he went back to Newfoundland three times a year was to see his parents and to see his child and make sure everything was OK. In fact, he had two families and was married to me and to Sarah White. It was so naive of me to believe his story.

"Ted and Ben, and Spencer too, you only had a father for three months of every year growing up because during the other time he was with his other family in Toronto where he had another wife and four children, my children. He never included Susie in his family. I will never forgive myself for abandoning our child, John."

Uncle John looked straight at her without saying a word.

Chen continued.

"Fred was rich, much richer than I ever knew until he left for the last time in 1989. By then, of course, all our children had grown into adults. He left a letter, in his own handwriting, telling me the truth about everything. He gave me half of what he had and divided the rest between his four children in Toronto. He told me he had looked after his child in Newfoundland as well. Of course, I always assumed there was only one child in Newfoundland. I never knew he married Sarah and had two children, until later."

Ted interrupted, "I'm sorry but this makes no sense to us at all." He looked at Ben who indicated he agreed with his brother. "Father looked after us growing up and always had enough money for the things that were needed, but there was no indication he was wealthy. And we certainly didn't receive any large sum of money when he died or before. Why should I believe what you are saying?"

"I can show you the letter he wrote me, if you wish. I

can introduce you to my oldest son, right by my side here, whose name is Fred, and my other boys Frank, Michael, and Hubert – he insisted on English names. I can show you pictures of us with the boys growing up. I can show you birth certificates. I can give you irrefutable proof if you need it," said Chen.

Ted and Ben looked at the man next to Chen and could see features of their father in his face. Fred bowed to them slightly and then looked back up, holding his head high. "Brothers," he said, indicating Ted and Ben.

"But I should finish," said Chen.

"After Fred left for the last time, I took over his business. It was a very large shipping company which was profitable, but a lot of his money had come because he used the shipping company as a front for smuggling and drugs. I closed that part down but discovered in my mature years that I had a better sense for business than Fred ever had. I've turned Hawkins Shipping into an international venture that is now listed on the Toronto Stock Exchange. I suspected Fred never ever gave his Newfoundland family much beyond what was needed. He did not want to raise suspicion if he came home with too much money." Chen paused as if she was tired.

"After Fred left and gave me and my children everything, I spent some years trying to decide what to do. I hired a lawyer and an investigator to find out what I could about Susie and John, and about Fred's other family. It is amazing what money can buy. I have been following all of your activities for years. That is why I knew about Susie and Jonathan's tragic end and was able to attend the funeral. I know about Uncle John's other child, Spencer, by none other than Sarah Hawkins. I know all about Ted and Ben and their families. And I know all about you Uncle John Parsons – if you fart, old man, I know it. It is amazing what money can buy."

There was silence.

Uncle John broke it.

"Why are you here today, really?"

"For a number of reasons," said Chen. "To unite all the pieces of this tangled family and to give you what Fred Hawkins never did – a share of his wealth."

"But it sounds like it is money gained through drugs and smuggling," said Johnnie.

"That source of the wealth is 30 years old now. What I have instructed my lawyers to give to the Newfoundland members of this family is from recent legitimate earnings," said Chen. "Please accept it as money that belongs to you as legitimate members of this extended family."

"Chen," said Uncle John. "Why now? What if you had died before being able to come here?"

"It was all arranged through my lawyers for you all to have received these monies on my death."

Ben now spoke up. "You said you and our father married in 1955. I believe that means the marriage to my mother was never legal. Father was a polygamist."

"Yes, I think that may be right. But also, since your father used a false name and birthdate on our wedding certificate, perhaps *our* marriage was not legal and only his marriage to your mother is. I have never bothered to investigate the legalities of it all. It doesn't matter to me."

"It might matter to us," said Ben. "If you and father were never legally married, then all his wealth may belong to us."

Chen's face went cold. "If you think I am not smart enough to have considered the possibility that you or your brother might take that approach, you are sorely mistaken. I can assure you that my ownership of Hawkins Shipping is air tight and the legal costs you would accrue in a challenge to me would bankrupt you."

"Please, Mrs. Hawkins, I am sure Ben was not implying that we would challenge you on any level," said Ted. "Ben just likes to look at all sides of matters. Isn't that right, Ben?"

"Yes, of course," said Ben. "I was not suggesting anything of the sort."

"Very well then," said Chen. "But there is something else that my story implies, and I have seen Johnnie and Penny talking to each other under their breaths. I believe you know what I mean."

"Yes," said Penny. "We know now that Susie Chen's real parents were you and Uncle John, my great-grandfather. We also know that Susie married Jonathan Ryan, whose father was also Uncle John, my great-grandfather and my husband's grandfather. That means that Susie and Jonathan, from whom I am directly descended, were actually brother and sister, or at least half-brother and sister."

"Yes," said Chen. "And that is what really brought me here today. I wanted to make sure you know that. I wasn't able to get here in time to tell you before you got pregnant and it is too late for an abortion now if you would ever do such a thing, but I wanted you to be prepared. You and Johnnie are not in the same situation as Johnnie and Charlotte were in, you are much closer related."

"Oh my God," said Penny.

"But," said Chen, "we know that Susie and Jonathan's child, Wendy, your mother, was and is perfectly healthy. And you Penny have not shown any indication of an adverse effect of consanguinity. I think the worst is over and the likelihood of danger from this unfortunate entanglement of genes no longer exists."

Penny looked at the old woman, "You think?"

"It is not what I think, child. It is what the best experts in the country think. I have consulted them all. I believe my great-great-grandson is going to be just fine."

"How did you know it was a boy?" asked Penny in surprise. "We just found out two weeks ago, and we haven't told anybody."

"Like I told Uncle John a few minutes ago – but to put it more politely – I am very well informed." She smiled.

Epilogue

On Saturday, September 21, 2030, at sunrise, Uncle John died at the age of 100 years. His entire extended family, direct and indirect, were with him when he went. It was the largest funeral Port. St. William had ever seen.

On October 30, 2030 Penny went into labour. She delivered on October 31, 2030.

They called the baby Sam.

THE END

Other Novels by Marshall Godwin

The Beothuk Series

Belle Maro

The Mark of Time

The Warm Place

Home to Liza

Charlie Freake

Look for them at www.felsenmeerword.ca

Manufactured by Amazon.ca
Bolton, ON